Praise for Peter Wood & *The Boy Who Hit Back*

"Easy to read and hard to put down, *The Boy Who Hit Back* is set in the recent past, but reflects the looming present. This novel is all about how tricky it is for people to connect in this new world of ours. Fame, love, drugs, death are all here and the ending—like those in real life—is sweet, but with an aftertaste of longing."

— Benjamin Cheever, Author of *The Partisan*,
Editor's Choice of the *New York Times* Best Books of the Year

"We're in John Green territory, without the tears, as a tough boy and a smart girl drag a punch-drunk fighter back to life and along the way make their own comebacks. Peter throws a sweet sentence and can knock you out with a paragraph!"

— Robert Lipsyte,
Author of *The Contender*

"Peter Wood's *The Boy Who Hit Back* is a story for anyone who ever wanted to take a swing at authority or dreamed of meeting one of the all-time greats of sport. This is a truly touching portrait of an intelligent, angry adolescent's redemption thanks to the magnetic allure of an ailing, broken-down former boxing champion, the ghost of the great Mickey Walker come to life."

— Ronald K. Fried of *The Daily Beast*
www.thedailybeast.com/author/ronald-k-fried

THE BOY WHO HIT BACK

THE BOY WHO HIT BACK

PETER WOOD

TCK PUBLISHING.COM

ISBN: 978-1-63161-052-3

Sign up for Peter Wood's newsletter at
www.peterwwood.com/free

Published by TCK Publishing
www.TCKpublishing.com

Get discounts and special deals on books at
www.TCKpublishing.com/bookdeals

Check out additional discounts for bulk orders at
www.TCKpublishing.com/bulk-book-orders

For my two beautiful muses, with love:
Sue Zhu and Zoe Makepeace

WARNING: THIS IS NOT A CHILDREN'S BOOK

This book is written for anyone who has ever screwed up.
Or was scared.
Or lost.
Or confused.
Or stuttered.
It's based on a true story.

Humpty Dumpty
Sat on a wall.
Humpty Dumpty
Had a great fall.
All the king's horses
And all the king's men
Couldn't put Humpty
Together again.

— A children's nursery rhyme

Chapter 1

W E'RE SITTING AT THE DINNER table concentrating on our lasagna when the storm hits. The house lights begin flickering, and rain — a hard, splattering, punishing rain — whips against the house. The wind moans. Suddenly, something upstairs bangs. Everyone jumps.

"That's Daniel's room," says my mother. The color is rising in her cheeks as she looks up at the ceiling. "I must've left his window open."

I didn't know anybody set foot into Daniel's room anymore. I sure as hell didn't.

"Matthew, go up and check," says my stepfather. "And wipe up any mess." That's my stepfather — a bossy jackass.

"Use a rag, dear," calls my mother. "There's a Handi Wipe beneath the bathroom sink."

I walk upstairs. I haven't stepped inside Daniel's bedroom in two years. Why should I?

My heart is thudding in my chest as I flick on the light. I'm half-expecting to find Daniel, my older brother, standing there grinning. But there is no Daniel or rain puddles on the windowsill, and his crap-colored shag rug isn't wet.

So I don't need the Handi Wipe.

I look around his room. Everything seems untouched—his Janis Joplin and Jimi Hendrix posters, his bed, and the photograph of his doo-wop group is still standing on his bureau. His two-piece Balabushka pool cue is still propped proudly in the far corner.

A wind-driven rain slashes against his window.

I slowly open his closet door. Daniel isn't hiding in there either. But I smell Old Spice, his favorite cologne. I poke around, behind his black leather jacket, to check his secret hiding spot where he stashed his weed. Not there.

Taped to his closet door is a photo of him two summers ago at the Jersey Shore. He's a handsome kid with a small mole, like a tiny chunk of tar, on his chin. In the photo, his Brylcreemed hair is slicked back in a duck-ass haircut, and he's wearing a tight bathing suit. "Hi, Dan," I say. "I'm your little brother, Matt. Remember me?"

"Get outta here," he snarls.

I shut the light and close his bedroom door. I don't miss my big brother too much, but my mother certainly does.

I take my own sweet time returning to the dinner table, which is set with delicate china, expensive silver, and artificial flowers. It's not my favorite place to hang out, especially when my mother and Jackass are sitting there. Four of us are at the table—my mom, Jackass, and Gram, my mother's mother, now living with us after the accident.

Daniel's seat is empty.

"...Europe is fertile grounds for franchising," lectures the jackass as I sit down. "Effective incentives...*blah, blah, blah*...and strict standards... *blah, blah, blah*...international law...*blah, blah, blah*..."

I zip my lip and choke down the lasagna in front of me, just quietly shoveling it in.

"Matthew," says my mother. "Your father and I—"

"Stepfather," I correct.

Oh, grow up, would you? says my mother's face.

Screw you, says mine.

"We received a call from your school counselor," she continues. "Apparently you had a little problem with another boy?"

"It's called a fight, Mom. I had a fistfight."

We sit silent. The wind and rain squirm and splatter against the windows like handfuls of gravel are being thrown.

I guess we're all waiting for the jackass to step into the

conversation and flex his tongue muscles. He slowly wipes his mouth with his white cloth napkin, places it on the table, and looks at me. "Tell us what happened, and in an orderly manner." He picks up his Liverpool pipe, which is lying beside his plate, stuffs it into his mouth, sits back, and waits.

"I hit a b-bully," I stutter. "He was stealing m-money from a freshman." I hate stuttering—it makes me look weak. I'm seventeen, and I inherited this embarrassing trait from my real father.

I think I'm calm, but beneath the table, I'm twisting my cloth napkin in tight knots. Twisting napkins and phony smiles are my method of dealing with the jackass.

"So now you're the brave savior slapped with a three-day suspension," says Jackass.

I look at his arrogant puss. He thinks he's so damn superior puffing on that nasty pipe. "Hey, Jackass, how many one-handed pushups can you do?" I feel like asking, but don't.

"In fairness to Matthew," says my grandmother, politely setting down her knife and fork, "when I met with the school principal, he confided with me—and this is not to be repeated, Matthew—he said he was proud of Matt for standing up to a school bully who has been terrorizing the school for four years."

My mother looks over at her new-and-improved second husband, a guy who wormed his way into her heart. He leans forward. "So, why are your grades dropping, son?" he asks.

"Don't know," I say. "This lasagna is terrific."

A cramped nervous smile appears on my mother's pretty face. "That's true, dear, your grades *are* dropping. Why?"

I bow my head submissively and continue choking down my terrific lasagna.

"Well, we expect a drastic improvement in your studies—and no more fighting. Is that clear?" he says, looking at my ear. Jackass never looks me straight in my eyes; it's always my ear or directly above my head. He has eye-contact issues.

My mother sighs with concern. "You were always such a good student who brought home excellent grades. And you certainly never got into fistfights. What's happened to you?"

What's happened to me is that I want to punch her pretty face and attack his arrogant puss.

Jackass places his pipe down onto the table. "Your mother and I expect to see an immediate improvement because, starting next month, you will be on your own. Your mother and I are traveling to Europe, spearheading new franchise possibilities…*blah, blah, blah*… working as a team…*blah, blah, blah*…setting up businesses…*blah, blah, blah*…and we won't be here to supervise you."

I grin. They're leaving!

My mother looks up at the ceiling, probably thinking about Daniel. He's monopolized most of her private thoughts for two years now, and she's become a perfectly perfumed mannequin—lifeless, emotionless.

Emotion has become her enemy.

We never talk about Daniel. And if we did, what would we say? It's too horrible.

Mom always wants everything to go smooth, to go right. But Daniel is the one who got away. I guess everyone's got a deep hurt inside them somewhere.

"Yes, I need a vacation," she says, biting her lower lip. She looks at Jackass for strength and comfort; he looks at my left earlobe for a response, and I look down at my terrific lasagna.

Gram stands up. "Dessert anyone?" She smiles, escaping into the kitchen.

Outside, the wind shrieks, rests, and shrieks again. The glass windows rattle, the lights flicker.

My stomach's killing me. I wanna punch something—anything.

Chapter 2

I MAY LOOK LIKE A normal kid, but on the inside I'm busted glass. I fake it good. I used to think I was okay, but since high school started, I began hating myself.

But ask me if I give a rat's ass.

Three years ago, in eighth grade, I was voted "Most Popular," and the kids elected me class president by a landslide. Girls loved me, I got good grades, and I'm an excellent athlete. So what's the damn problem?

High school is the damn problem.

I didn't decide to lose my popularity; it just flew away. Maybe it was all a huge mistake, me being popular in the first place. Reality kicked in, and everything began to slip away. The world doesn't revolve around me anymore.

But who gives a crap?

Not me.

So it's eight o'clock in the morning and I'm cutting school again. I'm sitting alone on the A train heading into downtown Manhattan. I'm so sick of school. School sucks. My family sucks too. But the root problem is *me*. I'm my problem. I know that.

Just give me a little time—I'll figure myself out. I'm a smart guy.

High school isn't hard. So why am I escaping it? Why am I sitting in this dirty subway car next to complete strangers instead of sitting in class with my classmates solving a stupid math problem?

Because *I* am my problem. That's why.

But, like I said, I could give a shit. I'll untangle myself one of these days, just you wait and see.

This crowded subway car is rocking back and forth, the lights are blinking on and off, the air is foul, and the brakes screech. I'm looking at all these sad old people going to work. But, really, I'm looking at myself looking at them. Yesterday, while reading *Hamlet* out loud in English class, I pretended I was Mimi Breedlove and watched myself through her eyes. Of course, I started stuttering.

Yeah, even in this subway car I'm looking at myself. It's a weird habit I have. I'm sitting quietly in the corner and I look like a healthy middle-class schoolboy from Closter, New Jersey—which, of course, I am, except for the healthy part.

Mimi, by the way, is the cute girl in the second row of my English class in Northern Valley Regional High School. I'm kind of in love with her. I'm a sucker for a pretty face.

"Excuse me," says an old woman standing in front of me, gripping two shopping bags. "May I take your seat?"

"Of course," I say, jumping up. "I'm sorry."

"Thank you, young man." She sits. "That's very kind of you."

She has a pretty face, but her paper-thin skin and stringy anorexic hair saddens me.

"Small acts of kindness," she says, nodding, "are always rewarded."

"I'm good at small acts of kindness." I smile. "Small acts of intelligence and courage—I'm good at those too. It's the big acts I have trouble with." Of course I don't say any of that. I just avoid her sweet motherly gaze and stare at the blackness of the subway tunnel.

All the way down to 125th Street she keeps smiling at me, thinking I am a warm, loving person. But honestly, I'm not a warm, loving person. I'm just good at pretending to be a warm, loving person.

My adventure into Manhattan on the A Train is always exciting. Even gray-haired old ladies, stale dead air, and disgusting subway rats are better than Mr. Buffington's geometry class. Most people think the subway is dreary and boring. But it's great theater. Last week I saw a man playing "Born Free" on the harmonica with his nose—only, he had no nose, just two nostril holes. Everyone felt sorry for him, including myself, and we dropped coins in his army duffle bag. Two weeks ago, I saw two women clawing at each other for a cinnamon bun that finally dropped onto the dirty platform. In February, I saw a filthy drunk fall onto the tracks. All that stuff is pretty sad, if you think about it. I remember a rabbi once telling me, "There but for the grace of God go I."

But today is the best — or worst.

When the subway door opens at 86th Street, a man and a woman, probably in their early thirties, enter. They're very businessy-looking, but the woman is walking the man on a leather leash. A *dog* leash. The leash is attached to a chain choke collar wrapped around the guy's neck. Both are holding briefcases, hers tan, his black.

She slowly trots him down the aisle, not smiling or anything. But they must be enjoying their weird show, even though everyone else ignores them and keeps reading their newspapers or sleeps.

They find two seats directly in front of me and sit down. She twists the excess leash around her fist and, as he attempts to sit beside her, she yanks it. "No!" she scolds.

He looks at her pleadingly.

"What did I tell you, Thomas?" she murmurs.

His wide eyes are like a naughty puppy dog's.

"Don't look at me like that!" she says.

"Please," he whispers.

"Heel!" She yanks.

"Please?"

"Obey!"

"Oh, c'mon," he whispers, thick with humiliation. I mean, a dog leash was wrapped around the guy's neck!

"I said *heel*!" she hisses.

He slumps down, squats on the floor, and rests his back against her leg.

She pets his curly brown hair and whispers, "Good dog."

I try not to stare. But it's hard. When a guy is sitting on the dirty floor of a subway car, wearing a dog collar wrapped around his scrawny neck, it's hard not to stare.

He doesn't bark, and she doesn't feed him a bone, but I have to peek at them every now and then. It's hard to find any real emotion on the man's face — or hers. It just isn't there. Every time the dog-guy catches me staring at him, I quickly look away. Our non-relationship exists only through our eyes. This whole thing is creepy.

"Are you looking at me?" he says softly.

I pretend not to hear.

"I said, are you looking at me?"

The woman pulls the leash. "Thomas! Behave!" She turns to me and says, "I'm sorry, he shouldn't do that." Then she yanks the leash again. "Right, Thomas? *Right*?"

He nods obediently. "Yes, Master."

He keeps staring at me. It isn't like he's going to bite me, but I feel pretty uncomfortable. I notice a slight curl to his thin lips.

As the door opens at 14th Street, she unravels the leash, yanks him up, and they head for the exit. Before they leave, he turns, grins, and says, "At least I'm connected to something."

"Thomas!"

His head yanks sideways and he is gone. But his left hand drops something that flutters to the floor. It's a business card. I pick it up and read THE PARADISE CLUB, 132 6TH AVENUE, 4TH FLOOR. "GET CONNECTED"

What's up with that?

Chapter 3

COACH SGRO, MY HARD-ASS FOOTBALL and baseball coach, yanks me out of Period 4 History to have a little chitchat in his gym office. I knock on his door, which is already open, and walk in.

"Sit down," he says, "and close the door."

He starts clearing off a pile of red basketball pinnies from a chair. His office is messy with football equipment, tennis balls, and racquets. Plaques and photos of past football players, basketball stars, baseball players, and wrestlers decorate the walls. Maybe I'll be up there one day. I'm a good athlete. That's a fact.

He sits square in his chair with both feet flat on the floor. "Know why I invited you down here?" He grins. It isn't a happy grin.

"No."

He reaches into his desk, pulls out a glossy piece of paper, unfolds it, and holds it up for me to see. It is December's *Playboy* pinup—a beautiful naked blonde lying on rumpled pink satin sheets.

"Recognize her?" he says.

"No."

He points to where someone had drawn with a black magic marker something very disgusting between her legs. It's pretty filthy.

He isn't grinning now. My heart begins pounding.

Coach Sgro isn't the type of guy to play with. His heart is a dry bone, and he has little tolerance for bullshit. He's a damn sadist who makes us run sprints till our legs puke.

"You sure this isn't your art?" he asks, gently folding it up and putting it back into his drawer.

"I didn't d-do that."

"That's funny," he says, pinning his gaze on me, "because it was hanging in the boy's locker room, next to your locker. Kids said you did it."

Unlike the jackass, who has an eye-contact problem, Sgro stares directly into my eyes.

"Honestly, Coach, I'm not lying. I n-never even saw that."

He sits there staring at me, saying nothing. I'm not sure he believes me — he knew my older brother.

"It's the truth, Coach! It wasn't me!" I don't want to start crying in front of my coach because, well, I'm a tough guy, and tough guys don't cry.

"Matt," he says, looking at me with concern. Then he puts his hand on my knee. "Are you all right?"

I nod.

"You're an angry kid."

I just look at him. He looks back at me.

"You're one of my best athletes, Matt. You had a pretty good football season, and baseball's right around the corner. I'd hate to lose you over something stupid like this."

"But it wasn't me. I swear! I'm not my b-brother!"

Billy Bickle did it! I know that for a fact!

As soon as the bell sounds, ending Period 5, I hunt Bickle down. I know it's wrong, but I'm spitting angry. I'm salivating to get my hands on that lying bastard. My good reputation is already shot, thanks to my older brother — and now this shit.

My mind is frothing. Hate and anger have been spewing outta me since Coach was ragging on me in his office. All during geometry, I've been digging into myself to find that feeling that's both calm and ferocious, and in the mud of my heart I find it. Festering in me is my crazy brother, my mother, and, of course, Jackass. They all generate a potent and poignant anger and hate.

I love anger and hate; it's such a good motivation.

When I spot Bickle walking down the hallway, I let sail a left hook. My full weight, shoulder, anger and hate are behind it. It splatters onto his face. I watch him crumble in pieces — feet, ankles, knees… As he falls, I drill him with a right uppercut. The punch catches him beneath the chin and bends his head back. He completes his downward crash — legs, upper body, and head.

I get suspended. Three days.

I'm doing a pretty good job ruining my own reputation.

Chapter 4

AFTER MY STUPID THREE-DAY SUSPENSION, I return to school to find the varsity baseball tryout list tacked up on the gym wall. All us baseball players are standing here looking up at it. The kid next to me is chewing on a stick of Juicy Fruit, judging from the smell.

BASEBALL TRYOUTS NEXT FRIDAY!
WHEN: 3:00
WHERE: UPPER GYM & WEIGHT ROOM
WHO: PITCHERS & CATCHERS IN UPPER GYM
FIELDERS IN WEIGHT ROOM
—COACH SGRO

Coach Sgro, you don't know it yet, but I'm your starting left fielder. I might get into a few fights every now and then, but I'm no screwball—like my brother.

The kid next to me turns and says, "You talkin' to me?"

"Nah, just myself."

Chapter 5

ENGLISHMATHSOCIALSTUDIESSPANISH – IT ALL SUCKS. So I skip school again. I'm good at skipping school, and Manhattan is the perfect place to skip to. It's a chilly, yet sunny, Tuesday three days before baseball tryouts and I'm strolling through Greenwich Village toward my destination — the Bowery. I feel comfortable and relaxed in my long-sleeve polo, jeans, and high-top Cons. I'm feeling just fine, thank you.

Freedom is the perfect antidote to school's rules and responsibilities. I mean, teachers suck. Why do they make school such a hell on earth? Yesterday morning, for example, the school nurse pulled me outta social studies for no good reason. "Are you taking any medication?" she asked.

"No," I said.

"Your social studies teacher tells me you're sleeping in her second-period class." As she was speaking, she was checking my eyes to see if I was dropping acid; I know that for a fact.

"Her class sucks."

She flashed her phony smile. "She says you rest your head on the desk."

"Class is boring."

"Well," she said, "let's take your blood pressure. Stick out your arm. "She was really examining my forearm for needle marks. I know that for a fact, too.

I'm sick and tired of getting pulled outta class because a teacher thinks my eyes are glassy or dilated. I'm fed up with a smiling nurse checking my arm for track marks. I know what they're doing. I'm not stupid.

I'm not Daniel.

In Greenwich Village, the shop owners aren't interested in checking my eyes or my arm. They're interested in sweeping and hosing down their dirty sidewalks. And office workers are too busy walking to work, drinking coffee, to give a rat's ass about me.

I'm as free as a bird!

The air is clean and quiet. Except for an occasional taxicab honk or the soft tire sounds of a delivery truck, I can hear a pin drop. I like being alone. There's nothing wrong with being alone. Even standing in left field, I'm alone.

Why am I heading to the Bowery? I have always heard the Bowery was a magnet for bums, the homeless, and sickos with a questionable grasp on reality.

Me? I'm totally at peace, walking alone with my high-top Cons slapping the smooth concrete. I think I might be searching for serenity. Most people find serenity from the majestic blue water of the sea or the flowing green grass of the country. Not me. Wandering alone with my own thoughts with no teachers, coaches, or parents screwing with me is fanfuckingtastic.

As I turn the corner, my poetic thoughts turn sour. I finally find my *serenity*—the Bowery.

The city shifts into a dingy black and white. It's like changing the channel and watching an old 1950s black-and-white movie—all grainy, jerky, and poorly lit. The droopy street is lined with bars, pawnshops, and check-cashing joints, all shut tight. Dirty old men are shuffling around. Some stare at me hard, while others sheepishly look away. I figure me walking all alone in this desolate place is a bit dangerous, and I do feel a bit nervous. Not everyone is friendly, and you never know who might want to hack you up with a butcher knife or shoot you with a semi-automatic. Hey, I'm only seventeen.

But scary is exciting.

Besides, I can handle myself. I'm a hard rock.

But what a disgusting dump! The place is thick with drunks and bums with unwashed faces. Some are sleeping on flat cardboard boxes, and some are huddled in groups, enjoying their morning smoke. Others, with bare feet, are just puttering around, stepping over dog shit and their own smelly piss from the previous night. I guess most of these guys have deep pathological problems.

Or they quit school and never bothered to return.

I walk down the cracked sidewalk looking at crooked noses, broken yellow teeth, old jagged scars, and brown facial scabs resembling burnt bacon. Something had gone horribly wrong in their lives. I study their faces and wonder what's going on inside their heads. What are their stories?

I hear Ms. Hanover, my English teacher, talking in my head. *Be kind. For everyone you meet is fighting a harder battle.* That's one of her pet sayings. Well, these sad men are casualties who had lost their battles and wars. But what were their battles? Perhaps I played hooky, taken two buses, the subway, and walked thirty minutes to find out.

I think I'm seeking serenity, but a voice in my brain is screaming, *Go home, Matt!* Another voice whispers, *Come join us. You belong here. This is what you want — serenity!* Hobos don't have homework or schedules or teachers and coaches checking your eyes or arm. Or a crazy big brother.

It's all mildly profound.

I want to talk to one of these panhandlers, just to understand them better — sort of like an anthropological study. "Why are you living down here? What's happened to you?" But that might be a bit nosey.

Finally, I stop in front of a harmless man with a flat nose. His weathered face resembles a well-worn nickel, and a cauliflower ear is popping out the side of his head. His hair, gray and oily, hasn't been washed in a decade. He's sitting on a stoop beside a smelly dog. Actually, they both stink.

He looks up at me and our eyes meet.

"George?" he slurs.

"I'm not George."

He squints. "Look like 'im." His pants and shirt are splattered with dry paint. I'm a tough guy, but somehow his vulnerable bloodshot eyes draw me in.

"Sir? I was wondering — "

"Ain't George? Then who you?" he interrupts angrily.

"Matt," I say, startled.

"How old're you?"

"Seventeen." I smile, but it isn't really a smile.

"Seventeen," he repeats. He thinks a minute, and then his lip curls into an ugly sneer. "Lemme ask you a question, boy. Why you down here?"

I'm stunned — that's *my* question to *him*!

Suddenly, his mutt stands up, wags its ratty tail, and staggers toward me. Immediately, I see something majorly wrong with its left eye—it's popping out two inches, like a wiener sausage. If I had a pair of scissors, I could snip it off.

"Why you comin' down here, boy?" he hollers, kicking the empty liquor bottle between his boots.

I look down at the old man, and then at his disgusting little monster, who starts rubbing its filthy fur against my leg. It probably wants to piss on me or give me rabies. I know I should've listened to myself and gone home when I had the chance. Slowly, the panhandler stands up.

I step back.

"Skedaddle, you!" He scowls and steps toward me, pointing his finger, like he wants to put some muscle into his message. "Lemme give you some valuable advice, George. *The two hardest things to handle in life are—*"

He suddenly bends over, coughing so hard I'm sure his kidney or lung is gonna fly out of his mouth. He tries to finish his sentence, but his voice wheezes out as if his throat is clogged with dust.

He wipes his eyes and tries again. "The two hardest things to handle in life are…" Suddenly, his eyes roll back, his knees sag, and he crashes to the pavement. His disgusting dog begins whimpering. Then it begins nosing around his head, licking the man's face. Then the mutt starts licking the blood flowing from the gash in the man's eyebrow. Sick!

The man looks dead.

"You okay?" I say, leaning over him. Suddenly, a door yanks opened and a guy from a bodega, holding a large pot, stands over the bum and pours water onto his head. The dog starts yapping, and the bum begins moaning.

That's when I beat it.

The Bowery is nasty!

I feel a lump of shame in my throat as I escape back to New Jersey. I sit on the bus taking me across the George Washington Bridge and look out at the gray water of the Hudson River rolling below. In the window's reflection I see a mixed-up seventeen-year-old kid seeking serenity, but instead found a poor old man who cracked his skull open on the sidewalk.

Millions of questions are squirming inside my brain, all talking at the same time and not shutting up:

What happened to that guy?

What was wrong with that mutt's eye?

What was his valuable advice?

What happened to my brother?

Would I ever have enough guts to ask out pretty Mimi Breedlove?

I'm so jam-packed with questions and, honestly, I have no answers. I shake my head with disgust and fish into my back pocket and pull out a card. THE PARADISE CLUB, 132 6TH AVENUE, 4TH FLOOR. "GET CONNECTED."

"At least I'm connected to something," that dog-guy had said — and he said it like he was the healthy one and I was the sicko.

Am I a sicko?

Today was so fucking profound. But don't ask me how. I have no clue.

I look out the window at the New Jersey Palisades, a line of steep cliffs plunging into the river, a national landmark. I have one more question: *Why did he call me George?*

That's my father's name — a man I haven't seen in over two years.

Chapter 6

GRAM LOOKS OVER HER SHOULDER while peeling Idaho potatoes. "Matthew, there's a postcard for you in the living room." I pick up a card lying on the mahogany table. It's from Copenhagen, Denmark. It shows a statue of a naked mermaid sitting on a rock with seagulls flying overhead.

Dear Matthew,

I'm sorry we left on such a sour note at the airport. Please know that even though your stepfather and I will be gone for a prolonged period, we love you very much!

I'm sure you will behave...blah...blah.... Baseball season is approaching and I trust you'll improve upon your studies. I'm so sorry we won't be there to cheer you on this year, but you're an excellent athlete and Coach Sgro adores you! Don't forget to help Gram around the house, cleaning dishes, taking out trash, making your bed...blah...blah...blah.

I love and miss you!
Mom

"Yeah," I whisper. "Sgro adores me—after he checks my eyes and arms." I rip her lousy postcard into a million pieces and dump it into the trashcan.

Chapter 7

Ms. Ping Hanover, my hotshot English teacher, dressed all in black, leans back in her squeaky chair and looks at me with disgust. She's tall, lanky, and Chinese. She rocks a long-ass ponytail, long arms, and wide shoulders. Probably early thirties. Gold necklaces are wrapped around her neck and a jade bracelet dangles around her wrist. High cheekbones and dark eyes. Yeah, she thinks she's hot shit.

She closes *Hamlet* and slides it across her desk. "Let me get this right, Matthew," she says, "you're skipping my class in order to hang out with the homeless in New York City?"

Stupid me! Why did I tell her?

She leans forward. "What are you, seventeen?"

I nod.

Here comes the lecture. She is an annoying English teacher who knows everything about *who* and *whom* and comma splices and writing essays, but can never understand a kid like me. Even though she rocks a long-ass ponytail, she's still an old coot. School has boxed her in for so long that it's shrunk her brain.

"I bet the Bowery hasn't changed much," she says. Then she looks out the window at the school courtyard where a thin maple sapling is blowing in the March breeze. "I haven't been down to that neck of the woods since *I* was seventeen. Describe it to me."

I tell her about the dead gray air, the bums sleeping on flat cardboard boxes, the stink of piss, and the disgusting dog with the wiener sausage eye.

"Still infested with the downtrodden, huh?" she says, seemingly to herself. Then she speaks in a British accent: "'I hate bums. I hate when I give them money, and I hate when I don't.' That's George Bernard Shaw." She looks back at me. "Well, mister, you missed your third *Hamlet* quiz. Did your Bowery buddies teach you anything about *Hamlet*?"

A clever response pops into my head. "Well, not *Hamlet*, but they taught me something else."

Her thin-penciled eyebrows lift.

"They taught me what *you* told us."

"Oh?"

"They taught me 'You gotta be kind. For everyone you meet is fighting a harder b-battle.'"

She thinks that through, and then smiles softly. "I've enlightened you! I'm, of course, merely the candle. Plato was the flame on that one."

Then she goes off — suggesting more profitable places for me to visit the next time I skip school: The Metropolitan Museum of Art, Central Park, The Guggenheim, a Broadway matinee on Wednesday afternoons. Crappy stuff like that.

"Thanks, but no thanks." I stand, grab my books, and slowly back out towards the door.

"What's up with you?" she asks, shaking her head.

I shrug. "I dunno." But it's none of your damn business anyway — you're just a teacher.

"Youth — too bad it's wasted on the young." She smirks, watching me walk toward the door.

But it's true. I'm not so sure what's wrong with me or why I'm visiting an ugly dump where old men walk, piss, and sleep on the sidewalks.

"You know, Matt," she calls out, "while you were down in the Bowery, Huckleberry Finn-ing it, you were lucky you weren't picked up for truancy. Yesterday, the Bowery was swarming with police."

"Why's that?"

"Sailor Barlow was found lying on the sidewalk."

I must have looked confused.

"Never heard of Sailor Barlow? The champion prizefighter? Wined and dined with kings and queens, presidents, and royalty from all over the world. Almost bled to death on the sidewalk."

Was my street bum Sailor Barlow? A famous boxing champion? His nose was pretty squished. "What's he look like?" I ask.

She looks at me so hard it hurts. "Don't be lazy. Research him."

Her swivel chair squeaks as she leans forward to pick up *Hamlet* and starts flipping through it. I guess it's her way of telling me our conversation was over.

I open the door.

"Matt…" she calls, rubbing the back of her neck and looking out the window, probably at that thin sapling. "Stop cutting school."

"Or I'll end up a bum on the Bowery?"

She doesn't answer. But her head is nodding up and down.

"Ms. Hanover, I already feel like a bum. I already see me lying on a flat cardboard box, panhandling," is what I feel like saying, but I'd never admit it. She's an old nerd with a long-ass ponytail, but she's a *kind* old nerd, and I can see a bit of concern for me in her pretty Chinese face.

"When can I take the makeup quiz?" I ask.

"You can't," she snaps. "You failed. Good-bye."

I close the door and pretend that I don't feel a tight knot in the pit of my stomach. Teachers suck the big one.

Chapter 8

I ENTER THE SCHOOL LIBRARY after lunch and walk past all the boring books and corny inspirational posters taped to the walls:

BE THE CHANGE YOU WISH TO SEE IN THE WORLD –Mahatma Gandhi

NOTHING IS IMPOSSIBLE –Audrey Hepburn

AS YOU THINK, SO SHALL YOU BECOME –Bruce Lee

Mrs. Roget, our evil prehistoric librarian, reaches up into her tight hair bun and plucks out a sharp yellow pencil. She's short, squat, and wears granny glasses that hang on a strap around her neck. She's always after me about shit.

"Hi, Matthew! I see you're here to pay your book fine?"

"Oh." I grimace, slapping my forehead. "I f-forgot."

"Again?"

I smile sheepishly. She doesn't smile back. I think my astoundingly good looks have stunned her.

"Well, the month of June is creeping up on us, young man," she says, tapping her annoying pencil on the wooden counter. "*Tempus fugit.* Time is fleeting."

"Tomorrow, Mrs. Roget. I promise."

She laughs, or snorts, and it isn't a pleasant sound.

"Drop dead, you old bag," I want to say. Instead, I go, "I'd like to do some r-research."

"On?"

"A boxer…Sailor Barlow."

"Ah, Benjamin Barlow!" she laughs. It's not a nice laugh.

"You've heard of him?"

"A real degenerate, that one. He was discovered lying on the sidewalk. I'd say it serves him right, but that would be mean-spirited."

"Why? What'd he do?"

"For one, he was a prizefighter who punched people for a living." she says." And two, he was a degenerate who developed an appetite for hitting animals—horses."

"I might've met him," I say.

"I certainly hope not! A monster like that?"

Monster?

She points her annoying pencil to the encyclopedias in the far corner. "Go do your research."

I walk past all her old dusty books—fat books, skinny books, hardcover books, paperbacks. Old Mrs. Roget didn't know diddlysquat. One day I was gonna write a great book, and the old biddy would be forced to buy *my* book and put *my* book on *her* library shelf. It would be a self-help guide for old teachers. I'd entitle it *How to Understand Students*. It would help clueless adults, to the extent that they could be helped, on how to encourage kids to read. It isn't that kids don't like to read; it's that we don't like reading boring books. I think our unwillingness to read is the result of us being force-fed crap that doesn't relate to us. No wonder we think books are ugly and horrible instead of exciting and cool.

Degenerate?

I pull out the *Encyclopedia Britannica* labeled B and cop a squat. Was my flat-nosed bum really a former champion, who wined and dined with royalty, or a degenerate monster? If so, what had happened to him? He spoke like marbles were stuck in his mouth, and his cauliflower ear was a beaut! I'm becoming intrigued by this smelly old man. And dog.

I flip through the encyclopedia: baseball...Basque Language... Birdman of Alcatraz...bonobos... boxing...but no Benny "Sailor" Barlow.

In a weird way, an encyclopedia is like the #84 bus or the A Train, because it takes you places. The cute girl sitting to my left is visiting the Mayan ruins of the Yucatan Peninsula in Mexico, and the pimply freshman on my right is visiting an ancient Greek temple in Sparta.

Nope—no Benny Barlow.

I look around for help. Teachers are teaching, students are studenting, and janitors are janitoring. School sucks. All I want is to identify Barlow's face.

In defeat, I bang my forehead on the table and plant it there. Maybe someday they'll invent a machine that will make research easy and fun—just press a few buttons and information will magically spit out before you.

I close my eyes. I'm feeling a bit light-headed and hollow, as if all my working parts are back in middle school and only my clothes, skin, and hair are here. I wish this damn encyclopedia could magically transport me back to eighth grade—before my parents' divorce, before my brother crashed and burned, back when I had friends, and back when my father was still around.

Sitting here with my forehead planted on the library table, I feel like a comet that dazzled on Monday but fizzled out by Tuesday.

I pull out another encyclopedia—S for Sailor.

Suddenly, my heart jumps. Sitting on the opposite side of the library is beautiful Mimi Breedlove. She's wearing a tie-dyed T-shirt, faded blue bell-bottoms, and pink flip-flops. Did she just glance over? Was that terrific smile actually for me?

Holy smokes! She's so hot!

Idea: Ask *her* for help!

It's easy: Stand and walk up to her. Right leg…left leg…right leg…left leg…Stick out chest…Flex muscles…Smirk…Talk. "Hi, Mimi. I'm wondering if you'd like to help me do a little research."

I walk over to her.

Right leg…

Left leg…

It's not easy approaching a cute girl.

Right leg…

Left leg…

Actually, Mimi isn't just cute—she's hyperventilatingly gorgeous. She's a seventeen-year-old female with incredibly thick, jet-black hair and big brown eyes that look deep into you. *Gorgeous* is a thousand times too weak a word to describe her. Why am I having such a hard time talking to her? I'll tell you why—because my mastery of the English language sucks. I mutilate most of my best thoughts by putting them into words.

Why can't I be confident like I was in eighth grade?

I walk closer.

Shoulders back…Stick out chest…

Mimi sees me coming, she's smiling!

Flex arm muscles…Chin up…

She's twirling her long black hair with her fingers. "Howdy, Cowboy," she says.

"Hi." I smirk. "Bye."

I stroll past her, real cool. On second thought, I don't need help from a girl. I'm strong.

Strong enough to walk away…but weak enough to look back. She is giggling into her fashion magazine. Well, I deserve it. I'm a frightened little punk.

I walk to the library exit. Right leg…left leg…I don't think she actually believes I'm the tough guy I'm pretending to be.

No, she's not buying it.

At the library exit I spot today's *Daily News*. I flip to the back page and read the headline "Lost Champ Found." Below the headline is a large photo of a prizefighter standing in the middle of the ring. A large battleship is tattooed on his chest and his muscular arm is raised in victory. His eye is bleeding, but he's grinning from ear to cauliflower ear. Yup! That's *my* Bowery bum…or degenerate monster.

I quickly flip to the inside article. "…Barlow almost bled to death before being rushed to St. Vincent's Hospital in Manhattan, where he remains in critical condition…"

Quietly, I rip out the article to read later.

What happened to him? A crappy childhood, I bet.

And what happened to his wiener-sausage dog?

For some crazy reason, I desperately need to find out.

Chapter 9

I SKIP SCHOOL THE NEXT morning and step onto the #84 bus.

"You again?" mutters the bus driver, a fat man, the spitting image of *The Honeymooners'* Ralph Kramden.

"Yeah, whatever," I say, throwing in my coins and grabbing my ticket. I find a seat in front.

He sneaks a quick peek at me in his rearview mirror.

I look like a normal kid — sneakers, jeans, and blue polo shirt with the collar popped up. I know, for a fact, guys think you're cocky if you pop your collar, but that's their problem.

It's early Wednesday morning, two days before baseball tryouts. I feel a rush of freedom, a tingle of maturity, but mainly a lot of shame and guilt. It's like a pebble's stuck in my shoe.

I should be in school.

The bus driver keeps reaching up to adjust his mirror to secretly look at me. I rest my head against the window as the bus pulls away from the cozy suburban towns of Closter, Demarest, and Cresskill. It's all behind me now — Mimi Breedlove, my sadistic football coach, my *family.*

"Nice day," I say to the bus driver, breaking the silence.

"Any day above ground is a nice day," he says, pulling into the small town of Tenafly.

I suddenly think of Sailor Barlow's words. "Hey, b-bus driver, if I asked you what are the two hardest things to deal with in life, what would you say?"

"My wife and...my wife." He laughs.

I laugh with him to be polite.

I reach into my hip pocket and pull out the *Daily News* article.

Lost Champion Found

Benjamin "Sailor" Barlow, the former World Light Heavy-weight Champion, the son of indigent alfalfa farmers in Arkansas, was found lying on the sidewalk in lower Manhattan...He held the crown for one year...After his wildly colorful, controversial and tragic boxing career ended, he attempted numerous unsuccessful comebacks. In later life, this popular sports figure became an oil painter who received considerable recognition as a primitive artist in New York City and Europe...Barlow has a history of alcohol and drug addiction, and suffers from dementia pugilistica. He was sent to St. Vincent's Hospital, where he was diagnosed with Parkinson's Disease, arteriosclerosis, low blood pressure, amnesia, anemia...He is 75 years old......He has no known remaining family...

I feel a tug at my heart. How can a former world champion sink so low? How many years has he been living on the streets? Barlow and I are as different as two human beings on this earth can be, and yet, I have a gut feeling that somehow this *monster* and me are connected.

The bus driver drives past Englewood, loops onto Route 4, and heads east toward the George Washington Bridge.

"Son, mind if I ask you a personal question?" asks the driver. He has a buzz cut, and it looks like he's forgotten to shave for a week.

"Go ahead." I welcome conversation because silence is sometimes awkward. I even catch myself starting stupid conversations just to avoid silence—like I already did.

"What's in New York?" he asks.

"Visiting someone...in the h-hospital."

"Family?" he says, eyeing me.

"No. Actually, the guy who said, 'The two hardest things to handle in life are... ,' but he never finished his sentence—a guy named Sailor Barlow."

He quickly turns his neck. "You mean *Benny* Barlow?"

"Heard of him?"

"Who hasn't?" he laughs with big amazed eyes. "Once won a boatload o' money on Barlow. How ya think I bought my wife's wedding ring? Bettin' on Benny! Haven't heard that name in years. In the hospital, huh? What happened?"

I read him the article.

"Oh, man! That's terrible!" he says, shaking his head. "The ol' horse puncher hit rock bottom."

"Horse puncher?"

"Yeah, some promoter set up this publicity stunt. Dressed Barlow up like a cowboy — big hat, leather chaps, cowboy boots — and told him to punch this horse, ya know, right in the kisser. So he did it! Hauled off and *socko*! Poor horse dropped! The gimmick was so successful he traveled around the country punchin' horses! Of course, it turned tragic."

"He killed a horse?"

"No — a *man*. Punched him to death in the ring."

I grimace.

"In San Francisco. All legit, but people called him a sicko and wanted him banned from boxing for punchin' animals. Sailor took it hard. I personally blame the promoter and ref."

Did Sailor Barlow punch his own dog?

The sun is rising, and I look up at all the dirty Fort Lee billboards soiling the early morning sky. I feel that pebble getting bigger. "Boxing's an ugly game," I say.

"Boxin' ain't no game, son. You *play* a game. Boxing's ugly, but Barlow made a lotta *pretty* money doing it. I was always a Barlow fan. You either loved or hated him. Young, handsome, and articulate — well, for a boxer, that is. Last time I heard, there was this photo of him all fat and bloated, trying to make a comeback in Mexico. Story was he asked the *policia* down there to lock him up."

"In jail?"

"To cut weight — eating only the pig slop they'd feed him in prison. Heck of a character, Barlow. Wonder if he ever lost that weight."

"He lost it, all right," I mutter.

"That's good. Maybe I should try that trick with the blubber-gut I got!" He slows the bus to the curb and opens the door. "Here ya are, kiddo — George Washington Bridge. Say hi to Barlow for me. And tell him he's to blame for my lousy marriage!"

"Okay." I laugh, stepping onto Lemoine Avenue.

"Oh, and another thing, kid," he says, looking down at me sternly. "You're a nice boy, but I don't wanna see you riding my bus again. Stop runnin' away from whatever it is you're runnin' from."

The pebble is growing bigger.

The blue-haired receptionist at St. Vincent's Hospital tells me Mr. Benny Barlow is resting in room 411 in Intensive Care. Before going up, I buy him a dozen red roses on sale in the gift shop. I'm sure his room is already full of flowers and get well cards, but what the hell.

I step onto the elevator, one of those huge ones big enough to fit a thousand gurneys. It's a slow ride up to the fourth floor, which gives me time to rehearse all the stuff I want to ask this former world champion.

What was it like to be a prizefighter?

What was it like to kill a man?

Why did he call me George?

What are the two hardest things in life?

The elevator opens. I turn left, check in with the nurse's station, then find room 411. I walk in. I'm a brave kid, but my palms and armpits are sweating.

Chapter 10

I T'S DARK INSIDE THE ROOM, and I see a thin man lying in a bed with protective metal bars raised on both sides. His arms and head are gently wobbling. Is this the correct room? Is this sad flesh-colored thing the same Sailor Barlow who punched horses and killed a man in the ring? I suddenly feel I have no right to be here and certainly no right to be staring at whoever it is.

But I walk closer. The man is lying on his back, and his hair is a mouse-gray crew cut. His flat nose looks like all the cartilage is missing.

It's Sailor Barlow.

His blank eyes are staring at the cracked plaster wall, and the bandage covering his right eyebrow is blood-soaked brown.

"H-Hello," I say.

He turns his head and looks at me. I wonder if he's still seeing "George."

I hand him his twelve red roses. He doesn't reach for them, so I place them on the metal tray attached to his bed, next to a plate with uneaten scrambled eggs. Under his flat nose I detect a small smile, and his eyes seem to moisten. "Beootiful," he slurs.

"Yeah, well...I read about you in the paper, and I thought, well, I'd come v-visit."

He squints up at me—a complete stranger. Even though he's an old man lying quietly in bed, his battered face would still give a young thug pause in a street fight.

I feel awkward staring at this former world champion—and I forget all the questions I had planned to ask. It's as if my stupid brain has amnesia. "I never met a world champion b-boxer before," I stammer. I hate when I stammer. People think I'm a pussy.

He looks down at the IV attached to the back of his hand. Then he gazes out the window, his head gently wobbling. Then he looks back and asks, "Was I a champeen?"

"Yes!" I say. "You were the light heavyweight champion of the world!"

He nods and looks at the cracked plaster wall. Then he turns his neck and stares out the window for a long time. I can almost see distant memories breathing within him. He glances back at me, our eyes briefly meet, and then he looks out the window again.

His body keeps wobbling, and the poor guy keeps staring out the window. Is he trying to remember who he once was? Am I embarrassing him? It's awkward and thick with silence. So I break it. "Mr. Barlow, you and I met b-before." I'm hoping his short-term memory will kick in. "You were sitting on a stoop, and this dog was beside you, and you stood up and said you were going to tell me something really important about the two hardest things to handle in life, and then you, ya know… fell down."

It might be crazy seeking words of wisdom from a street bum, but he isn't just any street bum, and my strong gut instinct tells me there's something important about his message and I need to hear it.

He looks at me, then out the window again. A gray pigeon flutters down and perches onto the brick windowsill, looks in at us, and coos. Barlow stares at the bird for a while, and then looks back at me. "You all by yourself, ain't ya?"

"Yes."

He studies me closely and says, "I c'n tell."

I don't say anything.

"You look lonely, boy," he mumbles.

"Me?"

"Yeah, you," he says.

In the center of myself, he's right, I *am* lonely. *Mr. Popular* in eighth grade is now a high school outcast escaping into New York City.

He looks down at his large hands. "Yeah…I remember now," he nods, inhaling deeply through his flat nose. He's a noisy nose breather.

"You remember me?"

"Yeah," he says gazing at the pigeon on the ledge. "I was a boxer."

"A world champion!"

"Yeah, had a few fights. One too many." He chuckles at the thought and looks down at his gnarled fists. "Know *why* I fought?"

I shrug.

"Guess." He grins, scratching his cauliflower ear.

I don't say anything.

"C'mon, George, guess. Guess *why* I fought."

I look down at his massive hands, and for some stupid reason they remind me of thick tree roots. This is all getting pretty weird.

"Guess, George," he insists. A bit of snot begins dripping from the tip of his mashed nose, and he wipes it away with the back of his hand. "You'll never guess."

For starters, I'm not a good guesser, and the hospital-y smell is beginning to annoy me. If anybody should be feeling lonely, it's *him*, with snot dribbling out his flat nose. I mean, this visit is becoming very awkward.

I shrug. "The money?"

"Nah," he mumbles, wiping his nose again with his pajama sleeve. "Guess again."

"The fame?"

"Nah." He chuckles. "Guess again." I can see from the smile on his battered face that he's enjoying this.

"I give up." The room is quiet. I hear the warm hospital air dragging in and out of his flat nose, and the nurses' squeaking rubber soles out in the hallway.

"I kept comin' back," he mutters, "'cause I missed gettin' punched."

"Excuse me?"

"I missed the closeness. The contact."

I look at the white worm-like scar in his left eyebrow, his chipped teeth, his battered nose, and his big cauliflower ear. There's a lot of *contact* on that face.

"Missed the human contact," he slurs.

I stand motionless and look out the window. A second pigeon joins the first, and they both look in at us, cooing.

"Ya see, when I figh' a guy, our souls kinda touch." He looks at the roses on the tray and reaches out to touch one. I notice the plastic tag wrapped around his hairy wrist. I never heard anyone utter a sentence like that—admitting he *wanted* to get punched. That he missed the *human contact*. I'm not a deep thinker, but I do a lot of intelligent feeling, and his wanting to get punched is sad and twisted. It's like that dog-guy in the subway wanting to be connected by a dog leash. My heart is beginning to cry for this sad old champion.

We stare at each other, and I break our silence by trying again. "Don't you r-remember *me*? When we met, you were going to tell me something important. You said, 'The two hardest things in life are…,' but you didn't finish the sentence."

He looks up and squints. "Remember? Remember what?"

"We met on the Bowery. You were sitting on a stoop with a dog."

He looks at my face for like eternity, squinting and nodding. "George," he says, "I'm sorry. I don't even 'member what I ate for breakfast."

I am trespassing. I am a young punk who belongs in school, not pestering an ex-champion recuperating in a hospital bed. I feel the pebble of shame.

I want to go home.

But before I leave, I want to put a smile on his battered face, so I ask him for his autograph.

His eyes are cloudy and confused, but he grabs the paper and pen I offer him and he scrawls his name. Even though he's wobbly, I notice there's a hint of athletic grace in his wrist, broad arm, and crooked hand.

After he writes, I shake his hand and notice his fingers are soft, like five big sausages.

"I gotta go now," I smile.

He suddenly reaches out and grips my arm. "You'll come back again?" he mumbles.

"Sure."

"Promise?"

"This weekend," I say, almost truthfully.

"You're a good kid." Then he lets my arm go and looks out the window at the two gray pigeons. "Thanks fer the roses, George."

I step into an empty elevator and press the down button. It's so sad: an old champ, his shaking body, and his drippy nose. He's a *degenerate* who wants to get hit. But that isn't the saddest thing. The saddest thing is there were no get well cards, and my twelve red roses were the only flowers in his room.

Before the elevator door opens in the lobby, I look down at Barlow's signature and my jaw drops. What he had written was pathetic, and it breaks my damn heart. I try to suck back my tears, but they begin running down my cheeks.

Chapter 11

SAILOR BARLOW, THE FORMER LIGHT heavyweight champion of the world, forgot how to write his own name. His signature is one, long, lonely, crooked line.

One fucking line! That's beyond sad.

Benny "Sailor" Barlow is now a harmless, confused, old man lying between two white Sanforized sheets staring at a cracked plaster wall.

Tempus fugit.

People are walking past me in the lobby, and I just stand here looking down at Barlow's pathetic signature. It didn't seem right — or fair. If he had died in the ring, he'd be a martyr, or an internationally famous sports hero, but now he'll probably die between those two white hospital sheets — a bum. A lousy forgotten bum.

As I walk onto the street, I don't really think he's a monster or degenerate and I have this crazy thought: I want to fatten him up and take him home with me. I'd bring him to school for show-and-tell, and he'd sit on Ms. Hanover's desk in front of class and tell us about his glorious championship fights, his smashing victories and gut-wrenching defeats. He'd sit by a window, and we'd learn about his hard-knock life in Arkansas, and listen to his hard-won wisdom as sunlight streamed down upon our young faces. At night, he'd sleep in my backyard, under a tree, in a nice bed I'd make up for him. I'd even bring my own L. L. Bean sleeping bag and join him. There's something nice about sleeping in the fresh air with the sky as your roof.

I ain't no sissy. I'm a hard rock, but I sometimes have these soft thoughts.

As I walk up Seventh Avenue, buses are honking and yellow taxicabs are swerving. Gray pigeons are pecking. The human traffic on the sidewalk is nurses, businessmen, deliverymen, and New School students. The only person my age is me. But that's totally okay. The beauty of New York City is that even in a crowd you're alone.

But I'm not totally alone. Inside my brain is a traffic jam: Barlow is grabbing my arm, teachers are looking at my dilated eyes, a nurse is checking for track marks, a stranger on a leash is grinning at me, a wiener-sausage dog is sniffing me, beautiful Mimi is haunting me, Coach Sgro is yelling at me, and somewhere at the back of my skull are my mom and dad and, of course, crazy Daniel, my older brother.

I look up at the fourth floor of St. Vincent's Hospital and wonder if the two pigeons are still checking in on Barlow. The poor old guy is so alone. I'm alone too, but I'd be damned if I'd let someone punch me or wrap a dog leash around my neck to be connected. That's sick.

The only thing Barlow is connected to is a lousy IV bag taped to his arm.

The two hardest things to handle in life are…

I wish he had finished that last damn sentence!

Life fucking sucks. I hate the way Sailor Barlow, a former world champion, has been tossed aside. I know that feeling.

I feel like killing myself. But I'm hungry and I want to grab a slice of pizza first.

Chapter 12

THE SMELL OF PIZZA INSIDE Ray's Original is insane. All these fancy slices in the glass showcase are making me drool: pepperoni pizza, chicken marsala pizza, Sicilian pizza, pizza with sausage, ziti pizza, pizza with ham and pineapple. Too bad I didn't steal more money from my grandmother's purse.

"One regular slice," I tell the guy standing behind the counter, "not too hot."

"Got'cha." He pulls open the oven, slaps in a slice, and shuts the door.

My mind is stuffed with sadness as I cop a squat. I look out on Seventh Avenue and spot a dead fly lying on the dusty windowsill. Would I ever kill myself? Why am I, now, wrestling with this stupid idea of death? Actually, jumping in front of a bus didn't seem so bad.

My brain hates me.

The TV up in the corner is showing an episode of *Lost Stars: Where Are They Now,* a weekly program featuring forgotten celebrities. This episode is former child star, Jane Withers. She's up there smiling from ear to ear. It must be nice to be resurrected.

I turn my head and look out the window at the hospital. Why am I so interested in this sad old man? Suddenly, I make the connection: me, my dad, and Barlow are three has-beens. We went from big juicy status to nothingness. The difference, of course, is Barlow and my dad, a once successful songwriter, are grown men who had already made the big show. I'm already, at seventeen, over-the-hill. I haven't proven myself in anything, except being voted class president and Most Popular three years ago.

"Slice!"

"That's me." I pick it up from the counter and look at the sizzling mozzarella. If there's one thing I fucking hate, it's when I say not too hot and they don't listen. If I ate this nasty piece of fire, I'd kill the roof of my mouth.

"Hey, you!" I yell. "I said not too hot!"

"Huh?" he says.

"You did it on purpose!" I shout.

"Whaddya, kidding me?"

"You're just jealous," I yell. "because you're a dumb idiot wearing a t-shirt and white apron and I'm a student, learning stuff, and when I graduate I'll be your boss." He throws off his apron and hops over the counter." And you hate yourself!" I add. That's when he picks me up, throws me over the counter, and stuffs my head inside the hot oven.

Of course, this only happens in my imagination. I'm always beating myself up. I do it ten times a day. I can't help myself. Self-torture.

I look back at the fly. He's still dead, but I mash him with my thumb anyway.

"Mind if I sit down?" says a pretty voice.

I look up and see a black woman wearing a pink uniform. The plastic tag clipped at her hip says "St. Vincent's Hospital."

I nod, blowing on my suicide pizza.

"Don't you just hate that?" she says, taking a seat, balancing a slice of spinach pizza in one hand and a bottle of water in the other.

"What? Sharing a table?"

"No, silly." She chuckles. "Blood-blister pizza."

"Yeah." I grin.

Her voice is sweet and sing-songy — probably Jamaican.

"Keep blowing, sonny," she says, pulling a paper napkin from the dispenser on the table. She opens the napkin and places it on her lap.

She stares at me. "Hey, don't I recognize you?"

I shrug, blowing. I wonder if it's my handsome face she recognizes or my wide shoulders or me crying in the lobby.

"Didn't you just visit someone in the hospital?"

I nod.

"Fourth floor?"

I nod.

"Mr. Barlow?"

"Yes."

"You the one brought flowers?"

"Roses."

She curves her mouth into a friendly smile. "That was so sweet. You a friend?"

"Kinda."

"Well, I'm Wanda, his day nurse."

"Hi."

She nibbles the tip of her pizza. "And you?"

"Name's Matt." I pick up my slice, but the damn thing's still too hot. I slap it back down. "How is he?"

"Mending."

"He was once a world famous p-prizefighter," I stutter.

"Oh? That explains his face," she says, patting her lips with her napkin. "He's a gentle one now. He likes me to rock him. He calls me Mama."

I grimace.

"He sucks his thumb, you know."

Suddenly, I ain't hungry. The thought of a former world champion sucking his thumb and unable to write his own name is beyond sad.

"Don't worry. He be fine," she says. "He's like a lot of the poor street vagrants we get. Quiet and respectful. But sometimes, you know, he comes out with the funniest things. Aren't you going to eat your slice?"

I shake my head.

She takes a sip of water and looks at me. "How come you not in school?"

I'm not too quick mentally, but I suddenly come up with a brilliant response—I change the subject. "Wanda, will you do me a favor?"

"Sure, honey. What?"

"If I wrap up my slice, will you give it to Mr. Barlow?"

"Well, I don't know. It's against rules."

"Aw, c'mon. It's just one little slice."

"Yes, I know, but our hospital has strict dietary regulations—"

"Please, Wanda. He's lying up there all alone with scrambled eggs he doesn't eat."

She looks at me intently as she sips water from her bottle.

49

"Please? One slice won't hurt h-him."

"Oh? So you a doctor now?" she says, narrowing her eyes. "It might burn the epidermis on his upper palate." She says it real high-and-mighty. I hate people pulling that holier-than-thou crap, trying to impress you with how smart they are. Besides, I know the meaning of *epidermis* and *upper palate*.

"Please?"

She looks out the window, up at the fourth floor, and then looks back at me. "Well, okay," she says. "But only on one condition."

"What?"

Suddenly, her sweet sing-songy voice loses all its pretty music, and she grows serious. "Promise me one thing."

"What?"

She puts her pizza down on her paper plate and leans across the table." Promise me you'll visit him again. Famous or not, that poor man ain't had no visitors till you show up."

"Yeah, I promise."

"Honestly, we don't know how much time he got left in this world."

"Does he have family?" I ask. "Anyone to contact?"

She shakes her head.

Life totally sucks — especially for Barlow.

I stand up, grab a paper bag from the counter, throw in my uneaten slice, add a few napkins, and hand it to Wanda.

She smiles. "I'm sure he'll appreciate this."

"Just make sure he doesn't burn the epidermis on his upper palate." I grin.

She grins back. "Wise guy."

"I'll be back this weekend," I say. This time I mean it.

Wanda walks out the door holding Barlow's gift.

I look up at a vase of flowers in a hospital window and feel confused. Why do I suddenly feel so happy and sad at the same time?

I look at the clock on the wall. It's time to head back home to New Jersey. I hate the thought of going home, but at least my mother and jackass are miles away in Europe. That's something to smile about.

But, Dad, where are you?

Chapter 13

GRAM DROPS HER DISH CLOTH and hands me a postcard. "They're in England." She smiles. The postcard shows "The Changing of the Guard" at Buckingham Palace. Soldiers are wearing big black fluffy hats, standing at attention like stupid idiots. I go up to my bedroom to read it.

Dear Matthew,

> *London is so beautiful...blah...blah...blah...Jack's unique, ready-made franchise system is... blah... blah... blah... We were extremely encouraged by our last trip to Dusseldorf... blah... blah... blah... Londoners are going "bonkers" over us!*

I love you!
Mom

P.S. Because of the tremendous response we're getting, we might be gone a bit longer than expected.

P.S. How many home runs have you hit?

"Mom," I mumble, "I ain't on the team. So I won't be hitting home runs this year." I rip up her postcard and throw it into the trashcan. Good riddance.

Chapter 14

Things are going more sour by the minute.

"So, you said a choke collar was wrapped around the dude's neck?" blurts Buzz. His lopsided smile makes him look stupid, and the scar over his eye makes him look tough. Stupid and tough—that's Big Buzz.

Actually, I gave him the scar last year—roughhousing in the locker room after football practice. The edge of the metal locker ripped his eye open.

We're sitting in the school cafeteria with Tommy and Little Gus. These guys are the only friends I got left. We always sit at our usual table cracking jokes on each other. They're juvenile delinquents, but funny juvenile delinquents, and they provide me with a lotta hard-core entertainment.

Our crazy friendship is based on sports, slap fighting, and insults—the more abusive and filthy, the better. Bullshitting with these guys is like a contact sport.

"Hey, Matt," chuckles Buzz, "tell us again about that dog's wiener sausage eye."

"Yeah, w-w-w-what's up with t-t-that?" laughs Tommy. His specialty is mocking my stutter.

These guys are, essentially, hoodlums who come from the mud of civilization. I know it was a big mistake telling them about Sailor Barlow's dog because they are the most toxic jerks in the universe, lacking any and all empathy or compassion. There's no minimizing their psychological development. That's a true fact.

But I still hang out with these lowlifes because they're jocks, like me, and maybe because I feel more confident around stupid people. It's better than being alone.

Big Buzz, our fullback, is proud of his mohawk and thick neck which grows out of his bulky shoulders. His body is the size of Trenton — but meaner. I call him "the ape who never evolved," but he can be a lot of fun to hang with. Tommy, our tight end, is a fast-footed, slow-thinking, lip-mover. Green-toothed Gus is our free safety. He's just a screwball with a shag haircut. He does a lot of sick stuff for fun — like shitting inside his brother's shoes and opening the lid of the A&P pickle barrel and pissing in it.

"I know why that dog's eye was sticking out," announces Buzz in a furry voice.

"Why?" asks Tommy.

"Barlow, the horse puncher, punched it."

I feel my cheeks redden. "Screw you, man."

Buzz grins. "*You* shut up, *M-M-Maryjane!*"

"Good one!" chuckles Tommy. I feel a quick spurt of anger. I know exactly what they're hinting at.

"If Barlow punches horses, he'll smack his dog," says Buzz.

"Smack…smack…smack. Get it?" laughs Little Gus. "Smack!"

I *got* it.

"Smacking a pet's pretty low," says Tommy.

"You're all assholes," I say.

"Yeah, but tell us how you really feel about us." Buzz grins.

Little Gus looks at me and smirks. "Matt doesn't like when we *needle* him."

"Or t-t-talk *smack*," laughs Tommy.

I stand up. I'm smart enough to know exactly what they're getting at and I don't like it. "I don't know why I sit with you jerk-offs."

Tommy yanks my sleeve to sit down. "C'mon," he says "You're one of us!"

The thought of being connected to them is hurtsome.

"You think you're better'n us," spits Buzz. "Don't ya?" Buzz might be 210-pounds of raw muscle, but I'll kick in his face if he keeps it up. Sometimes you have to show guys you can hurt them, otherwise they'll walk all over you. That's a fact.

Suddenly, Buzz lowers his head, and mutters, "By the pricking of my thumbs, something wicked this way comes."

A hand touches my shoulder. "Matthew, may I see you a moment?" I look up and see Ms. Hanover's angry Chinese face. She motions with her thumb. "Outside."

Buzz grins. "See ya later...*Maryjane*."

I follow Ms. Hanover into the hallway. I know this is going to be a ten-minute lecture on how I'm gonna end up a bum if I keep skipping school. I start thinking of a quick excuse about why I cut her class yesterday.

I fake a cough.

She looks at me like I'm a stupid liar, which, of course, I am.

I cough again — harder.

"I thought I made it very clear to you," she says. "No more cutting."

"Ms. Hanover..." *Cough.* "Let me tell you the reason why —"

"No. Let me tell *you* the reason why," she says. Then comes her lecture.

I pretend to listen. It's more advice shoved down my throat. She lectures about wasting my potential...blah...blah...blah...and running away from my problems and failing English.

I cough.

She lectures about bad habits and how bad habits are hard to break, and respecting myself...blah...blah...blah..."Look at me when I talk to you!" she snaps.

I look at her. Yeah, whatever. I cough.

She lectures me about how junior year is the most important year for colleges, and about finding decent friends, and me wasting a perfectly good education, and if I mess up, it's my fault — not my parents'...

This is getting very annoying. I don't want to waste another minute of my life listening to an old English teacher with a long ponytail like a horse tail. I'm getting an earache.

I look back down at my high-top Cons.

"Matthew, look at me! I'm sure it must upset you about your brother, but you still have to move forward."

"You don't have to get personal, Ms. Hanover," I say. Does every teacher at Northern Valley Regional High School need to remind me about my crazy fuckin' brother?

She tilts her head. "Okay, go back to your friends and enjoy lunch. But know this: 'One's real life is not the life one always leads.'"

What the hell does that mean?

I walk back to my juvenile delinquents.

It was a cafeteria table when I left, but now it's a freak show. Buzz's leather belt is wrapped around Little Gus's neck, and Tommy is feeding him French fries.

"Arf! Arf!" barks Gus, pretending to be a dog. He's sticking out his tongue and lapping up fries Tommy feeds him. The only thing Gus doesn't do is wag his skinny butt. Kids watch them with horror.

When Buzz sees me coming, he picks up a piece of broccoli. "Hey, *Maryjane*—here's a pretty flower for Mr. Barlow!" He says it girly-like.

Tommy and Little Gus laugh. But it isn't very funny.

Buzz stands up and shoves me and, boy, I don't like being shoved. He has the wild eyes you see sometimes in a bucking horse, and he holds the stare. I hear him breathing in and out, his chest is heaving up and down. My palms start sweating, my heart begins pumping, and the back of my testicles are shriveling up. I hate when that happens. "Giving a guy roses?" he spits, "That's fuckin' gay."

Buzz's hands are curled into fists. A fight is seconds away.

A fistfight draws kids—even honor roll students like to watch a good fight. It's more entertaining than Shakespeare. Buzz is just staring at me, planning where to plant his fist. "What're you—a faggot?" he growls.

I glance quickly over his shoulder and I see Mimi Breedlove. Her wide eyes are freaking out and she's holding both hands over her mouth.

Chapter 15

BUZZ'S SNEAKERS ARE PLANTED TWO feet from mine. Tommy and Little Gus stand behind him, struggling to look just as dangerous. My heart is pounding and my mouth is bone dry. I'd feel much braver if I wasn't so scared.

I'm looking at Buzz's jaw, thinking left hook.

"What're you—a faggot?" he repeats.

I grin. "Why? You looking for one?"

My witty response inspires nervous laughter. But, the next thing I know, I'm flat on my back with a 210-pound fullback kicking, clawing and choking me to death. The boy's on fire. I feel the strength in his massive arms and muscular back as he squashes my face flat into the linoleum. It hurts. With a gut-wrenching, muscle-screaming twist, I swivel around and manage to push his face up by his jaw and land a few punches, but that's when the scumbag drops his head down and sinks his teeth into my chest. I scream.

The psycho bit me!

He might be bigger, but I'm faster and smarter. I quickly jackknife my legs up over his head and end up sitting on his chest. This switch isn't too good for his self-esteem, but it works wonders for mine. Once I untangle my left arm, I begin pounding his ugly puss. When his nose breaks, he shrieks.

"Hey!" shouts a voice. It's Coach Sgro bulling through the crowd. "You fightin' again, Watt?"

"Just horsing around, man," squawks Buzz, wiping the blood dripping from his nose.

Coach isn't buying it. His eyes are narrow slits as he glares at both of us — mostly me. The vein in his forehead looks like it's ready to explode.

Mr. Colantoni, our short cocky principal, is waiting for us in the school office. He stares at me, his hands on his hips. "You fighting again, Watt?"

"Good to see you too, sir," I say.

"Don't be a wiseass," he says. He looks over at the blood dripping from Buzz's busted nose. "Get him a towel!" he yells.

A secretary runs to the bathroom.

"Well," says Colantoni, "I guess I can tell who won this fight."

Buzz flips him the bird while wiping blood off his lip. Colantoni misses it.

"He called me a faggotty bitch," says Buzz.

The principal looks at me.

"He bit me," I say, lifting up the bottom of my shirt to show him the bite marks. Colantoni bends down to get a better look. Then he looks up at me. His face says, *You're walking down the same road as your older brother, kid.*

"Sir," says Buzz, wiping his face with toilet paper the secretary handed him. "did you *not hear* what I just told you? He called me a faggotty bitch. How'd you like it if I called you a faggotty bitch?"

Colantoni slaps him across the face. "Shut your trap, Broadnax! I've had quite enough of you this year!"

Broadnax does exactly that — shuts up.

"Boys were fighting in the cafeteria," clarifies Coach Sgro. He looks down at me and shakes his head. I'm toast.

Suddenly, Ms. Hanover walks in. Her thin penciled eyebrows lift when seeing Buzz's bloody face.

"Fighting in the cafeteria," explains Coach Sgro. He looks at me and shakes his head again. "Should stick to playing ball, Matt."

Ms. Hanover looks at the principal with concern. "There's a mistake."

"Mistake?" says Sgro.

"Matthew was with me."

Coach shrugs. "Maybe. But he was also rolling around in the cafeteria floor punching Broadnax."

"I don't get it," says Ms. Hanover, holding up her palms. "Matt was with me a few moments ago."

Colantoni stands there giving it great thought. He rubs his hand over his face, but doesn't say anything. It's the longest silence I ever sat through. His uncalm black eyes just stare at me, then Buzz, like we're war criminals. I don't like a principal staring at me.

"Mr. Watt, you hang with Broadnax, right?"

"No more."

"You lie down with dogs, you rise up with fleas." He jerks his head toward his office. "Get in! Both of you!"

"You kidding me?" I scream. "I ain't going in your stinking office! I did nothing wrong!" Of course I didn't say that, but I wanted to.

I quietly follow Buzz into Mr. Colantoni's office.

Chapter 16

IT'S EARLY FRIDAY MORNING AND I step onto the # 84 bus. I scrounge into my pockets for the nickels, dimes, and quarters I had stolen from Gram's purse earlier this morning. After counting, I drop a dollar fifty into the slot.

"You again?" says the bus driver, shaking his head. "You're breaking my heart, kid."

"Whatever." I don't mean to be rude, it's just that I'm not in the mood to be friendly to Ralph Kramden this morning.

He studies my face and laughs. "You kids're the smartest people in the world — you got all the answers."

"Look, Ralph, stop giving me lip or I'll drop you!" I wanna say. Instead, I politely grab my receipt, stuff it into my back pocket, and sit in the middle of the bus.

Colantoni slapped me and Buzz with a two-day in-school suspension. Buzz can jerk off all day in that cinderblock jail cell if he wants. Not me.

Colantoni signed me up for an anger management program, which is where you basically sit around with a bunch of losers and bullshit being mad.

Well, I got better things to do. I know it's insane, but visiting a washed-up prizefighter who enjoys getting smacked in the head is my *better thing*.

For some reason, I'm latching onto Benny "Sailor" Barlow and playing baseball this season doesn't seem quite as important.

I look out the foggy window and can't see where we are or where we'd been—Cresskill maybe, or Tenafly or Englewood. It's cold and dreary as I watch raindrops cling nervously to the outside of the window. Occasionally, a raindrop drips down and connects with another raindrop, then another, then another, till they become one big, fat, friendly raindrop and slide off the window and die on the road.

Friendship is overrated. Friends always hurt you in the end.

I look at one tiny raindrop hiding in the corner. It didn't connect with other raindrops. It's strong and independent. Why connect with other raindrops? So you can get big and fat and slide off into the road and die together? I think not.

I once had lots of friends. Whatever.

Once upon a time, friends enjoyed hanging out at our house—that's until Daniel got busted selling maryjane—and then smack. My friends stopped coming because they got sick of my mom and dad screaming and fighting. Yeah, there's still a lotta heavy gloom in our house, and hanging out with me isn't fun anymore.

My social slide first began when I entered high school. Kids started to mature—but I stagnated. The eighth grade prez and Most Popular was now in the rearview mirror. Ms. Hanover once said in class, "'Every hero becomes a bore at last.'" I wrote it down in my notebook because it relates. I can't blame anyone but me for screwing up these past three years.

Hey, too much thinking sucks.

I sit here chewing the inside of my cheek. I'm sick and tired of my own confusion. I know deep down something is wrong with me, but I can't put my finger on it. And I'm not gonna talk to no counselor, like they want me to. Maybe I was born negative. Or bipolar, or schizoid, or dyslexic. Maybe I'm mentally ill and just don't know it yet. Maybe I'm manic-depressive or have chicken pox in my head.

There are a lotta of things I don't know. I don't know if there are UFOs. I don't know if there are ghosts. I don't know if there is a Bigfoot in Montana. I don't know if there is really a Bermuda Triangle. I'm pretty sure there is no Loch Ness Monster in Scotland, but how about crop circles in England? I don't know what's at the end of the universe. Heck, it's so smoggy outside, and I don't even know if we are in Cresskill, Tenafly, or Englewood.

I *do* know Mantle is better than Mays, but I don't know who I am, and I don't know what I will become.

Northern Valley Regional High School doesn't give me answers to these big questions. In fact, school just feeds me more complicated questions. "One's real life is not the one we necessarily live" is a perfect example.

I look at the window cluttered with raindrops and see a distortion of myself. Why am I so fucking unconfident? I slap the window, and the raindrops jump off. I'm discovering that it's impossible for me to attend high school and not be full of confusion and self-hate.

Suddenly, something small hits my head. I turn around. A few seconds later, something small whizzes by me. Then something wet hits my earlobe. I stand and look around. On my right is a middle-aged woman in a gray business suit reading the *Daily News*, and two seats behind her are a black man and a white woman, both sleeping.

I sit back down and it happens again — something soft and mushy, like a spitball, hits my ear. I stand again and look for psycho Buzz. Not there. I sit back down and someone taps my shoulder. "Hi!" says Mimi Breedlove, popping up. "I was scrunched down below — right behind you!"

"I k-knew that," I lie.

"Did not!" she laughs. "Mind if I sit next to you?" she asks, plopping down beside me. She's wearing a pink hooded sweatshirt and faded bell-bottoms. I can smell coconut shampoo in her thick black hair, which falls past her shoulders and gleams with a thousand brushstrokes. I wonder if she irons her hair, like some girls do.

Why is she on the bus? I'm about to ask her, but she cuts me off.

"Those boys, yesterday in the cafeteria, they were such jerks! Were they mocking you?" She tilts her head and combs her long hair with her fingers. I notice her fingernails are red-raw — bitten to the nubs. "They're your friends, aren't they?"

I look away, embarrassed. "No more."

"It's okay if they are. I mean, you sit with them every day."

"Yeah, well, that's because, I mean… they're on my f-football team." It's funny how I can talk to an old boxer, but talking to a beautiful girl gets my heart sweating.

"That's okay," she says, digging at a red-raw cuticle with a fingernail. "Friends are friends. But, wow, with friends like them, who needs enemies?"

I shrug. "Yeah, w-well…"

"So, how come you're ditching school?"

I tell her about my two-day jail sentence and try sounding tough doing it.

She nods and looks out the window. While she combs her hair with her sore red fingertips, I fidget nervously with my bus receipt, tearing it into little strips. It's uncomfortable silence. We sit here just listening to me tearing my ticket.

"So, this is a coincidence—me and you sitting on the same bus. Where you going?" she asks.

"New York. I'm visiting someone in the h-hospital."

"Oh, I'm sorry. Who?"

I stammer through my crazy Barlow story: his sick dog, him falling down, the bloody pavement, the dozen red roses, him wobbling in bed, his sad flat autograph, Wanda the nurse, and my gift of pizza.

She looks out the window and got thoughtful. She came upon a particularly bothersome hangnail and begins biting it aggressively. I hope my stuttering didn't turn her off or that I didn't say the wrong thing. Maybe she didn't like me now. Maybe I am just a moron—like my toxic friends.

"Thick or thin?" she asks.

"What?"

"What kind of pizza—thick or thin?"

"Thin."

"I *love* thin pizza." She smiles.

We laugh a bit and then look out the foggy window again. I wonder how I am doing, conversation-wise.

We grow quiet. I hope we aren't talked out. I mean, what if we have nothing in common?

She looks back at me. Her beautiful brown eyes are full of thought and her wide mouth is perfectly lip-glossed. "Now I understand why that boy was holding that piece of broccoli, mocking you," she says.

I shrug like it doesn't bother me, but it does. I hate being mocked. Getting mocked is the worst thing in the universe. It's like death.

"I think you're sweet," she says, "bringing that poor man roses, and then giving him a slice of yummy pizza."

I shrug. "Wanda probably ate it. The flowers are probably dumped in the garbage can."

She looks at me weird. "I've noticed you have a very negative mind-set. But you are," she touches my arm softly, "capable of being very nice."

I swear, when she touches me, an electric shock zooms up my shoulder and down into my balls. It's like a sweet lightning bolt. All she did is gently touch my arm with her red fingertips and *wham!* — electricity rips through my body. That's never happened before. It's... wonderful.

We both look at each other, then out the window.

On the window I notice the raindrops running together, playfully mating, getting larger and swollen. I want to kiss her, right then and there, on her pink glossy lips.

I move closer and our thighs touch.

Chapter 17

I'M A BIT NERVOUS AND don't have the guts to kiss her. That's because breakfast was scrambled eggs, four oatmeal cookies with milk, and I forgot to brush.

"Foggy, isn't it?" she says, squinting out the window. She reaches across my chest with her left arm and begins swishing the window with her palm. Her shiny black hair brushing against my cheek feels like satin, and the smell of coconuts smells like hope. I know that's poetic, but—I shit you not—it's giving me a wicked boner.

"Yeah." I nod.

"Yeah, what?"

"It's foggy." Like my life, I almost add.

She sits back. "I don't get it. Why were you suspended? You were defending yourself."

"Well, if you l-lie down with dogs, you rise up with fleas." I shrug, adjusting myself.

"But he attacked *you*."

I shrug again.

She picks at the red-raw cuticle on her thumb. "So what did your parents say?"

I shake my head.

"You told them, right?"

I rub my nose, scratch my ear.

She punches my arm. "The school called your house, right?"

"Were those spitballs you threw?"

"*Flicked* them," she corrects.

"Good aim."

"My father taught me. We had spitball fights all the time." She looks out the window and smiles. I think it's a smile, but it doesn't reach up into her eyes. "I once flicked a big fat wet one into his mouth."

"Yuck!"

"That's *exactly* what he said — *yuck.*" She rewards me with a smile, but it's a faint smile, and more at the foggy window than at me. "We used to play around a lot like that."

I see her smiling, but I think I see something hidden behind it.

The bus is slowing down, getting ready to drop us off on Lemoine Avenue. It's the most magical bus ride ever — me and gorgeous Mimi Breedlove talking and laughing.

"So? What did your parents say about your suspension?"

"Not much." I shrug. Everyone has parents — that's inevitable, but I don't wanna tell Mimi how I had divorced mine two years ago.

She looks at me weird.

I don't want to tell her my parents are a pair-of-ants — small and insignificant, and living in two separate ant holes far away from me. Besides, the bus has stopped and people are walking off.

"How about you?" I ask.

"How about me what?" she says, standing, turning her back.

"How come you're not in school today? You never said."

"Because you never asked," she says, walking down the aisle, exiting the bus. Once we hit the pavement, she turns around and faces me. She looks upset. "You know what I think, Matt?"

"What?"

"I think you're self-centered."

"Huh?"

"You're self-absorbed."

I look at her.

"I asked *you* many questions. You asked *me* one."

"Yeah?" I say. "So?"

"You're a narcissist."

Narcissist?

"You're just like my last boyfriend — all wrapped up in yourself. My friends were right. You're selfish. I thought you might be different. I actually wanted to get to know you, but you know what? I was wrong."

She turns and starts walking away. I follow her. I can't believe what I'm hearing. It was going so good between us. "I don't like negativity," she says, walking faster. "And you're a depresso-narcissist," she adds, over her shoulder.

"Am not!"

"Are too! You're always slouching in the school hallways, looking down at the floor. Sadness is written all over you, and it splashes on everyone else. You smell of negativity."

Is she a psycho or what?

At the corner, she hangs a left and I follow her. She stops. I stop.

"Screw you!" she blurts.

I look down at her red-raw fingertips nervously fidgeting with the strings of her pink sweatshirt. Yeah, something is definitely bothering her.

"So," I smile, trying to turn it around, "where you going?"

"That question doesn't count."

"I'll walk with you."

"Get lost!" Her eyes begin tearing up, and she turns and walks faster. Yeah, something is eating her up. Something's wrong. What's her secret?

"You're stalking me!" she shouts. "Just leave me, the fuck, alone, you depresso-narcissist!"

"Mimi…I *like* you." I want her to like me back.

Tears are rolling down her cheeks and she's catching her breath in long choking gasps.

"Where you going?" the depresso-narcissist asks.

"Get away from me!"

"What the..!"

"I *hate* you!" she screams, running across the street. I watch her run. In my heart of hearts, I knew this was the door-slam waiting for me from the very beginning. I turn around and look up at the billboard in the fog. A beautiful woman's face in a Clairol hair-conditioning ad is looking down, laughing at the depresso-narcissist.

What's a depresso-narcissist?

Chapter 18

THERE HE IS, THE MIGHTY Sailor Barlow, lying in a fetal position. The room is dark, his eyes are shut, and his thumb is sticking in his mouth. For the first time, I notice, he isn't wobbling. Despite his battered face, dented nose, and scarred eyes, it looks like he might be having sweet dreams.

But he's dead.

Yeah, something's majorly wrong. There's an absolute stillness to his thin body. Gray whiskers are covering his face and neck, and I read somewhere whiskers and toenails keep growing after you die. If he is dead, at least he's dead in a clean bed, not on a dirty sidewalk.

I got to admit, I don't like touching dead people, but I wanna touch him just to see how cold death is.

"What? No pizza today?" says Wanda, switching on the light. I jump.

"Oops! Sorry if I scared you." She's wearing her pink uniform and squeaky white shoes. Her hair is perfectly braided, and her chocolate-brown skin shines in the fluorescent light from above.

"He's dead," I say, feeling a lump in my throat as soon as I say it. Tears will be next. I hate when I cry. I'm a tough guy, so I clench my teeth and fists, and scrunch my toes inside my sneakers. It's a trick I learned dealing with my asshole brother and lost father.

She smiles. "It's naptime." She fluffs a pillow and places it against his side. "I be nursing twenty years and seen a lotta dead people, and

I promise you, Mr. Barlow ain't dead." She shrugs. "Shouldn't you be in school?"

"How come he ain't shaking?" I say, cleverly changing the subject.

"His nervous system sleep too. As soon as he wake up, he'll shake a bit. But his tremor be improving."

"But he's dead," I whisper.

She smiles. "Don't you worry none, sonny," she says, bending down to clean up the breakfast spilled on the floor. "Mr. Barlow's blessed with one of them slooow athletic heartbeats, is all. He's progressing nicely. I even took out his IV yesterday morning. Notice?"

I look down at Barlow's flat face. There's no drool or nothing. "Holy smokes, Wanda! Look at him! This is so damn sad…Excuse my language."

"I will not!" she says. "Your language is fucking disgusting."

We grin at each other.

"Trust me, dearie, you don't know sad," she says. "I use to work the children's ward, with boarder babies. Their home be this hospital. Now *that's* sad — infants abandoned by their mothers — drug-addicted, usually. We hug and cradle 'em. If we don't, they be yellin' and screamin'. They want human contact. Wanna go visit 'em downstairs?"

I shake my head.

"Well, then, I'll tell you what you be missing. Bright-colored wallpaper with smiling bears and cute pink bunnies. You see shiny thingies hanging above each crib. Infants lying in them cribs — yellers and criers, mostly. Then there's the head-bangers, they be craving attention so bad, they bang their heads till you pick 'em up. Then you got the vomiters — crafty little monkeys. They be so dirty, we forced to hold them to clean 'em up. Then you got the quiet thumb-suckers, they just stare into space. Sure you don't wanna visit?"

I shake my head. I'm here for Barlow, not boarder babies. Besides, the brown and yellow hospitaly smell would really stink.

"Don't blame ya, dearie," she says, shaking her head. Then she looks down at Barlow's dead face. "So, what I be saying is Mr. Barlow's sittin' pretty. He's forgetting some words, but his memory'll improve some. Hey, he's already enjoyed a nice long life."

Had Barlow's life really been nice and long? Sure, he was a world champion, but if he wanted people to hit him, how enjoyable could it have been? I look down at his scarred eyes, cauliflower ear, and thumb stuck in his mouth. It's like he's an *old* boarder baby. Poor guy. "What happens to boarder babies?" I ask.

"Orphanages, adoption agencies, foster homes..." She looks over at the cracked plaster wall for a moment and says, "With the proper loving bonds, anyone can thrive. You know, he ask about you all the time now."

"He does?"

"Last night, after *All in the Family*, he says, 'Where's that nice kid, George?'"

"Name's not George."

Wanda smiles. "He thinks it is. He gets confused, but someone bring you red roses and pizza, you remember 'em."

I study his face. I'm looking for movement, a twitch or fluttering eyelid. I've seen dead people on TV and that's exactly how they look — dead. "You sure he's not dead?"

She shakes her head. "This morning, he remembered a girl's name — Lavender."

"Wanda, I think he's dead."

She looks down at Barlow and sighs. "Oh, okay, let me check to see if you be dead, Mr. Barlow." She leans down and studies him. Suddenly, her eyes widen and her hand shoots up to her mouth. "Oh, my heavens!" she gasps, leaning closer. She tilts her head one way, then another, examining his dry, lifeless face. She squints like she overlooked something vital, and reaches up to hold her hand close to his nostrils. "Well," she says, "Mr. Barlow, you the prettiest dead man I ever seen."

Grinning, she squeaks out the room. At the door, she turns. "If you wanna wait till this dead man wakes up, go ahead. *Sport Illustrated's* over there."

I'm still not entirely convinced. He hasn't moved a single damn muscle. Wanda might be wrong. Is Barlow in a coma?

I sit here watching Barlow's dead face. I feel like a disappointed kid visiting the lions at the zoo when they're asleep in their cage. When I was young, and my dad took me to the Bronx Zoo, I was always tempted to reach into their cage and pull a tail, but he told me it wasn't a good idea. I guess I am selfish, just like Mimi said. But the truth is, I want to help Barlow. I just don't know how. If Barlow had a tail, I'd definitely pull it.

I sit here, waiting for him to wake up.

I think about boarder babies. Is Barlow becoming one?

I flip through *Sports Illustrated*. I bet his picture was once on the front cover. My father was once on the front cover of *Billboard*. Dad isn't famous like Barlow, but he once had made his tiny splash in the music world as a composer.

To kill time, I count the white tiles on the hospital floor. I count them a second and third time, just to be sure I was right the first time. Then I do the same with the hangers in the closet. Then I recount the tiles.

Ten minutes pass.

Then I do what I did when I was a kid. After my parents' divorce, every other Saturday morning, I'd wake up early and sit in front of the big picture window, waiting for my dad's Plymouth to roll into the driveway. Me and my packed suitcase would be waiting for our court-adjudicated weekend together. I'd count: 10...9...8...7...6...5...4...3...2...1... He's coming around the corner right...now!

It never worked. He never came.

I look at Barlow and begin counting: 10...9...8...7...6...5...4...3...2...1...

He's going to wake up right...now! I count five more times before I quit.

Getting bored, I walk over to Barlow and look down at his dead face. How can a stupid kid like me help a former world champion? I have an idea! And I'm not gonna let this golden opportunity slip through my fingers. Maybe I can't find my dad, or pass geometry, or be Most Popular again, but I can help this damaged old man.

I decide to punch him.

One small punch. A quick little smack on his jaw. That might shake him out of whatever coma he's in. I won't hurt him. Just a little love tap. Nothing hard.

I'm not a psychologist, but I think a little poke to his jaw might actually do him good. Shock therapy. Tough love. Didn't he say he liked to be punched? Well, a little love-tap from a seventeen-year-old kid is harmless, compared to shock therapy, which, by the way, blows out your fucking brains.

I stand over Sailor and look at his battered face. He's been punched a million times already, probably lost a gallon of blood, and one more tiny smack won't hurt. I just wanna help this forgotten hero. He's all alone, like me. Didn't my crazy football coach always tell us, "No pain— no gain"?

I lean over, clench my fist, and aim for his jaw. If Wanda walks in and sees this, she won't understand, so I have to do it quick.

I raise my arm and swing.

Chapter 19

SMACK! His eyes snap open.

"I'm s-sorry, Mr. Barlow," I say, nervously. "I just wanted to see if you was dead."

Struggling, he pulls himself into sitting position. "Ya wanna play rough, huh?" He lifts his hands up like a fighter. "C'mon, you little twerp!" He grins.

I can't tell if he's happy or pissed off. But there's a big red welt on his cheek where I smacked him.

I raise my hands and we start slap-boxing, because, well, that's obviously what he wants. It's so damn weird. A moment ago he was dead, and now he's full of life. It's so cool seeing a big smile appear below his flat nose as I try to slap his cheek. But I never come close. His reach is long and he's surprisingly quick. He begins belly laughing whenever I get cute and fake with a left and throw my right.

"Ooohh!" he mocks.

I switch it up—faking to his face and going for his stomach.

"Aaahh!" he laughs.

He's real quick for a guy who was dead a few minutes ago.

I feel like a kitten pawing an old lion. I step closer…

The next thing I know, I'm sitting in a chair with Wanda pressing an icepack onto my face and my head is throbbing like a bad tooth.

"You okay?" she gasps. "I walk in the room and see you dumped on the floor!"

I look at Barlow. He's pouring ice water onto a towel and tosses it to me.

"What were you two doing?" asks Wanda, looking at Barlow, then me.

"Horsing around," I say, blinking my eye.

"Horsing around?" she says. "I thought *you* was dead!" The thought of seeing myself on the floor, knocked out by a professional boxer, makes me laugh. When Barlow sees me laughing, he starts laughing, and it sounds like dry crackers are stuck in his throat. Then Wanda starts laughing a high sing-songy laugh. Even though we're all laughing at me, I don't mind. I haven't laughed so hard in three years.

"If I had to guess," says Wanda, examining my eye, "your left eye hit Mr. Barlow's right fist. Am I right?" I shrug. The cold icepack on my eye feels good.

"What're your parents gonna say when they see this here eye?" she asks with concern.

"Don't worry," I say, blinking. "They're vacationing somewhere in Brazil or China."

She looks at me weird, then at Barlow. "This ain't gonna happen again, understood?"

Barlow nods.

"And I mean it," she says, pointing. "That's no way to treat a fine young boy who bring you flowers and pizza."

Barlow smiles. "Thanks for the…" He struggles to find the word.

"Flowers?" prompts Wanda. Barlow nods.

"No problem," I say.

Barlow motions to his mouth. "And the…"

"Pizza?" says Wanda. He nods.

"We all have senior moments," she explains.

Barlow looks over at me with concern and mumbles, "You okay, George?"

"Yeah," I nod.

"I was wonderin'," he says, "can you get me…"

"Another slice of pizza?" asks Wanda.

"It's down the street," I say standing up, holding the icepack. "I don't mind."

Barlow shakes his head.

"More flowers?" she asks.

He shakes his head again. His forehead wrinkles with frustration. Wanda and I stand there, waiting for him to find the words. It really sucks being old and punch-drunk.

"Lavender," he finally mumbles. "Can you find Lavender?"

"Your wife?" smiles Wanda.

He shakes his head.

"Your daughter?" I ask.

There's a look of deep pain in his face. His expression is full of words, but he can't come up with them. Hey, finding the right words is my big problem, too.

He reaches for a pad and pencil on the tray and starts writing. He holds the pencil sideways, like an artist sketching. As he writes, I notice his body isn't shaking too bad.

After finishing, he hands me the pad. On it is a sketch of a dog.

"Lavender is a…dog?"

He smiles big, and his gnarled hand reaches out to hold my hand.

"*My* dog," he mumbles. "Please find her." He closes his eyes and lifts my hand to his cheek.

Chapter 20

I STICK MY HAND IN the mailbox and pull out a postcard showing the pointy Eiffel Tower lit up at night. I go upstairs to my room, close the door, jump on my bed and read the scrunched up handwriting.

Dear Matthew,

Paris is breathtaking! It's saturated with beautiful art and important history! Versailles is exquisite! Jack and I visited the Louvre yesterday and viewed a marble statue of Narcissus. It brought me to tears because it reminded me so much of my two strong, handsome sons. Dies Gram need to remind you to do your daily chores and homework? I trust you are behaving like a perfect angel while we're gone.

All our love,
Mom and Dad
P.S. How many homeruns have you hit this week?

"Mom, I'm not hitting homeruns, but I think you struck out with a Freudian slip—you meant to write *does* not *dies*." I throw her postcard into the trashcan.

Chapter 21

Early Saturday morning, I hop on the #84 heading to New York, then catch the A Train heading to Greenwich Village. I'm on an important mission: find Lavender. I know it's gonna be impossible, but I can't just sit around and do nothing when I know there's no one else to do it.

Somehow, nosing around New York City to find a wounded dog has become more important than hitting homeruns.

Pretty girls are walking into handmade-jewelry stores and Sam Goody's record shop. Hare Krishnas are singing and dancing, and a noisy pet store is selling monkeys, little green parakeets, blue parrots, golden geckos, and big fat iguanas. What the hell is a gecko?

Greenwich Village is jam-packed with crazy stuff. I see a poet with green hair sitting on a dirty red stoop. I know he's a poet because he's writing a poem with a long quilled pen while smoking a joint. A musician is strumming a guitar, his skull is dyed purple. A tall thin girl wearing a pink tutu is walking five dogs down the sidewalk. Greenwich Village is wild and edgy and everyone seems to be a budding artistic genius on the verge of stardom. You'll never find this cool stuff in Closter, New Jersey.

I pass the Café Wha?, The Village Gate, and The Bitter End, famous coffee houses for singers like Bob Dylan, Dizzy Gillespie, Richie Havens, plus a million others. Then I turn right and retrace my steps to the Bowery.

"Hey, boyo!" calls out an old gypsy woman dressed in black. She waves me closer. Her bracelets are noisy and every finger is ringed. She's sitting on a chair and behind her is a painted board showing a hand with a life line, heart line, and a red love line. "Boyo!" she says, looking at my face. "I see a very dark shadow falling over you!"

"Shut up, lady."

She probably noticed my black eye—it's a beaut. Everyone's admiring my black eye, all puffy and purpley. Actually, I'm very proud of it. All us hard rocks suffer a black eye once in a while. That's life in the big city. How many guys can claim they were slugged by a world champion boxer?

"I warn you, *boyo!*" she calls out.

"Get lost, fruitcake."

Boyo is on an important mission to rescue a wounded dog. I even brought my Kodak Instamatic to snap her picture—just in case I do find her.

I walk south, out of Greenwich Village, toward the Bowery. Where the green trees, poets, pretty girls, and dreams end, the Bowery begins. Boy, if my mother saw me down here she'd have a heart attack.

Sitting on a concrete stoop is a panhandler talking to himself. The poor guy has pee stains on the front of his khaki pants, and his teeth are stained brown. His whole world is probably stuffed in the large plastic garbage bag sitting beside him. There but for the grace of God go I.

He's too old for violence, so I'm not scared to approach him. "Excuse me," I say, "do you know Benny 'Sailor' Barlow?"

He tilts his head. His long oily hair is tousled and twisty. "You mean the horse puncher?"

I just look at him.

"A real sicko, him," he says with a proper British accent.

"Have you seen his dog?"

He blinks his eyes. "Have...I...seen...his...dog? Dog is god spelled backwards."

"She's called Lavender."

He starts snapping his fingers at two imaginary dogs he's hallucinated into existence. "Here, Lavender! Here, Chartreuse!"

Something is majorly wrong with this guy.

"Are you hotdogs or colddogs? Are you even dogs?" he asks. Behind his serious face is pure insanity. "*Pardon, monsieur,*" he says, switching to French. "Do you have a spare *franc*?" He holds out his hand and I dig into my pocket and drop a quarter into his palm.

"*Merci!*...Franc...franc...frankfurter," he says, tapping his left arm furiously with his fingers. "Is there *franc* in a frankfurter? Of course there is. Is there ham in a hamburger? Ask the FBI, they know. We're all trapped in a spider web. Ha! Ha! Ha!"

I walk away fast. This isn't the best neighborhood to be alone in, but I need to find Lavender. What if I do find her? Bring her home? Wouldn't my grandmother love that!

On the next piss-stained block, where I had met the Champ, sits another bum. He's thin as poverty, and he's leaning against a brick wall with a big piece of canvas cushioning his butt. Faded tattoos cover his arms, and a crusty scab's on his forehead. "Haven't eaten today," he says, looking up at me. "Starving." His watery eyes are pitiful and his filthy feet are bare. When he reaches out to me, I notice three fingers and two stumps.

I hand him a quarter.

"God bless you, sir," he says, dropping the coin into his shirt pocket.

"Do you know Benny 'Sailor' Barlow?" I ask.

"Yeah," he says, coughing.

"You do? Do you know his dog?"

He coughs and nods.

"Lavender?"

"You mean Popeye?" he wheezes.

"No. Lavender."

He starts coughing so violently that a yellow clam flies out of his mouth and lands on his foot. It looks like a plop of butterscotch pudding dripping from his toe. It's disgusting. Then he tucks his head between his knees and coughs even harder. After recovering, he hocks up another plop of pudding and spits it out. "Lavender's too pretty a name for that beast," he mutters.

"Where can I find her?"

"Horrible mutt," he says, wiping the tears from his red, watery eyes. The poor guy is struggling to catch his breath as he digs into his pocket for a Chesterfield.

"Where can I find her?" I repeat.

He points to a saloon across the street. The Blarney Stone.

I walk across the street, open the wooden door, and walk inside. What am I getting myself into?

Chapter 22

I T'S DARK INSIDE AND IT smells like I just stepped into a dirty ashtray. There's a long bar on the right, and a line of tables running down the middle. On the left are high-backed booths, a jukebox, and celebrity photographs hanging on the walls. The place looks exhausted.

It's empty of people except for two old geezers sitting in back watching *The Price is Right*.

"Well! Well! Look who's here!" says a voice.

I turn my head. The bartender is looking at me with no expression — just standing there, polishing a shot glass. "It's Huckleberry Finn, the classic underachiever."

It's Ms. Hanover, my English teacher, standing behind the bar. She's wearing a Yankee cap, pulled backward, and her black ponytail is twisted into a long horse braid. The sleeves of her red plaid shirt are rolled up to her elbows.

She continues staring at me. Or glaring.

I say hello without stammering and look down at the sawdust on the wooden floor.

She just stands there, arms crossed, staring at me.

It's so weird seeing a teacher outside of school, but seeing your English teacher in a sleazy bar is creepy — and too coincidental.

"What am I doing here, right?" she says.

I shrug. Shrug? Christ! A shrug is eloquent. I was on a roll.

"I live down here," she says.

I walk over and slide onto a bar stool.

"Whaddya have?" She smiles, polishing the bar with a white rag, slowly rubbing back and forth.

I shake my head. "Nothing."

"Nice eye," she says, pointing with her chin. "Where'd you get it?"

I tell her about my new friend—Sailor Barlow.

She grins. "Ah! So you finally met Benny, huh?"

"You know him?"

She looks out the window and points. "Benny lives across the street. Up there—second floor. Two-C, to be exact." She looks back at me and snaps her rag in the air. "He popped you good."

I nod.

"So now you know my dark little secret—I moonlight for extra cash. Times're hard." She puts her elbows on the bar, leans forward, and studies my eye. "Benny's normally a pretty peaceful guy. You must a been buggin' him."

I explain about him looking dead.

"Poor guy's hurting, huh?"

"Nurse says he's getting better, medical-wise."

She nods.

"So, you wanna tell me what *you're* doing down here?"

I'm not the smartest kid, and even though I've been me my entire life, I don't understand myself too good. Sometimes my motivations, like tree roots hidden deep under dirt, aren't so clear. So I just sit there, shrug, and look at the brick wall behind the bar. Actually, I'm very much a mystery to myself, and my brain is sometimes silent and thick, just like that brick wall.

"I'm looking for a dog," I finally say. "Sailor Barlow's dog."

"Ah, Popeye." She laughs, polishing the bar in a slow circular motion.

That's when I notice the tattoo on her forearm: BORN TO RAISE HELL. English teachers aren't supposed to have tattoos. I guess that's why she always wears long-sleeves in school.

She notices me staring.

"Oh, that," she laughs. "Students ain't supposed to see that. A token of my misspent youth."

"How old were you when you got it?"

"About your age. I hung with the wrong crowd." She stares at me.

I get the hint.

"The tat was supposed to prove I was tough." She laughs. "I was a young asshole seeking friendship in all the wrong places — pardon my French. I guess back then, I was a follower. I lacked some type of… emotional muscle. 'The bird a nest, the spider a web, man friendship.' That's William Blake."

Even though we're not in school, Ms. Hanover is still stuck in teacher mode. I don't mind. There's something comforting about it. But I'm still surprised she's even down here, tending a sleazy bar.

"Matt, strong people don't get inked to broadcast how tough they are," she says.

"Don't worry, Ms. Hanover, I'm not getting a tattoo, and I don't hang with those bozos anymore."

"No judgment," she says, studying my face.

She picks up a beer glass, holds it up to the light, inspects it for spots, and then begins polishing. I guess Ms. Hanover isn't so bad after all. I'm seeing a different side to her. *One's real life is not the life one always leads?*

In back, a spoon starts clinking against glass. She looks at the two men in back and answers the call with a sly grin. "Two liquid breads, comin' right up, boys!" She says it James Cagney-ish. She grabs two Rheingolds, cracks them open, and walks them to the back table.

In class, she's always switching voices to keep students interested. Sometimes her voice is Edgar Allen Poe or Scout Finch. Sometimes she even rips on our short Napoleonic-complexed principal, Mr. Colantoni. She does a pretty good Kurt Vonnegut, but my favorite is her Edna St. Vincent Millay — she really makes those old dusty poems dance.

But there's something dangerous or pathological finding her inside this dark smelly place. I can't put my finger on it. Why is she really here? I always thought people walked into a bar feeling sad and then walked out happy. But I don't see anybody getting happy. The two burnouts in back are liquored up already, and they aren't smiling.

What's her secret?

Behind the bar is a photograph that grabs my immediate attention. It's Sailor Barlow wearing an artist's beret and smock. He's standing in front of a painter's easel, wearing boxing gloves. Clutched in one glove are three long paintbrushes and clamped in his teeth is another brush. Paint is smeared on his cheeks, hands, and smock, but there's a smile of contentment on his face. He's in the process of painting a dog that looks a lot like Lavender — without the wiener-sausage eye, of course. The bold signature at the bottom reads: To my pals at The Stone — Benjamin "Sailor" Barlow.

I'm studying the photo, when the wooden floor behind me squeaks and a hand touches my shoulder. I spin around. It's one of the old geezers. "Well," he says, smiling, "you're a pretty good-sized fella."

"Who's got a damn good left hook," I spit.

He raises his hands. "Whoa! Relax!" He's tall and thin and is wearing a white dress shirt. His emerald-green tie is long and thin. "You know, son, you look awfully familiar."

"Does," nods the smaller man with fat yellow teeth standing beside him. On his nose is a crop of disgusting blackheads.

They both study my face as I look back at Sailor Barlow.

Green Tie points with his Rheingold. "You know Benny?"

"Could'a been a famous painter," says Fat Teeth, "if he painted without boxing gloves." "Shut up," says Green Tie. He then points his bottle at my swollen eye. "What happened, son?"

"Benny hit him," explains Ms. Hanover from behind the bar.

"He *hit* you?" gasps Green Tie, sliding onto the bar stool beside me. I nod.

"Must'a been a peach of a punch!"

"A lucky punch," says Ms. Hanover, helping me out.

Green Tie leans closer. I smell beer and cologne. His thin gray hair touches the back of his collar. "Well, then," he says, "it's perfectly obvious what your black eye signifies!"

"Freddy," says Ms. Hanover leaning forward. "Don't start."

"I will too start!" he exclaims. He reaches out and pats my shoulder. "This strong young man is connected!"

Ms. Hanover stands there watching, quietly polishing a beer glass with her rag.

"Connected to what?" says Fat Teeth.

"Must I explain everything to you insufferable clodpoles?"

Ms. Hanover looks like she's ready to explode. "Okay, Matthew, it's time for you to go."

I hop off the stool and start walking to the front door.

Green Tie grabs my arm. "Come back here, young man!"

Chapter 23

THIS HANDSOME YOUNG SQUIRE IS now officially connected!" exclaims Green Tie. His voice is a deep baritone, full of authority. It's surprising for a guy so skinny.

"Connected to what?" says Ms. Hanover.

"To American greatness!"

"I'm warning you, Freddy," she says, slapping her rag on the bar. "Leave the boy alone." There seems to be a clenched fist in her voice.

"Eat my knickers!" says Freddy.

Ms. Hanover grits her teeth and her face turns deep red, the color of a Crayola crayon.

They glare at each other.

"Don't look at me in that tone of voice!" says Freddy, pointing with his beer bottle. "This young lad's connected to one of the most masculine and virile heroes in modern-day American sports, and someone has to tell him!"

"Shut up," growls Ms. Hanover. She plants her hands on the bar and leans forward. "Just shut up!"

"I shall not just shut up!" hollers Freddy, stamping his shoe on the floor. "He needs to hear it!"

Ms. Hanover's Chinese face is ready to burst. "Matt," she says, "you don't belong here. Get out."

"No! I demand you to stay!" He points to my eye. "That is not merely a black eye—it's a medal! I'll explain," he says softly. "The great Jack Dempsey, the world heavyweight boxing champion in nineteen thirty—"

"Nineteen twenty-six," corrects Ms. Hanover.

"Yes, you are absolutely right, Professor Ping. I stand corrected. In nineteen twenty-six, Dempsey punched heavyweight champion Jack Sharkey—Sharkey punched Primo Carnera—Carnera punched Max Schmeling—Schmeling punched Max Baer…you following this? Baer punched the great Joe Louis—Louis punched Sailor—Sailor punched Matt! Get it? This young lad's connected to boxing royalty!"

Me—royalty? I kinda like the idea.

"I'm sorry," he says. "I haven't properly introduced myself." He stands up and straightens his green tie. "I am Fredrick Ambrose Covington."

"Or Funny Fred," scoffs his friend.

"And this imbecilic little cur is Norman…And your name is?"

He's not the boss of me—just because he told me his name didn't mean I had to tell him mine. I look at Ms. Hanover, whose red cheeks are now a quiet pink. She nods.

"Matthew Watt."

Funny Fred turns to Ms. Hanover. "Professor Ping, I'd like the honor of buying a beer for my new friend, Matthew Watt."

Ms. Hanover stares at Funny Fred and doesn't move. "Control yourself, Fred, or someone else will," she warns.

"I hear you, Professor," says Funny Fred, "loud and clear."

Ms. Hanover pours me a drink and slides it over. "*Root* beer," she says, leaning onto the bar with one elbow. "After you finish, you should get going."

I pick up the frosted mug and take a sip. It's ice cold and delicious. It isn't like I've never drank *real* beer before, but the root beer feels good going down—cold and sweet. Actually, I'm flattered by Funny Fred's speech about me being connected to all those boxing champions.

That's when the phone rings, and Ms. Hanover walks to the back end of the bar to answer it.

"Nice camera," says Funny Fred, pointing to my Instamatic. I explain about wanting to snap Lavender's picture.

"You mean Popeye?"

I nod.

"Never find her," mutters yellow-toothed Norman.

"W-Why not?" I stutter.

"It's impossible."

"Why impossible?" asks Funny Fred.

He grins, sipping his beer. The rim of his glass touches the top of his nose, and he politely wipes the beer scum off with the back of his hand. Impeccable etiquette. "Because she likes Chinatown, that's why."

"Norman, don't dash the boy's hopes," says Funny Fred. Then he turns to me. "I'll help you find Popeye. I know her favorite spot — Broome Street."

"Too late," says Norman. "She's dead. Chinks ate her."

"Can it, Norman," snaps Fred. Norman grins. "She's already rolled up in a dumpling. Chinks eat cats too, ya know."

That's when the front door opens, and in shuffles the thin three-fingered wino from across the street. He parks himself onto a bar stool, slowly reaches into his shirt pocket with his claw, and carefully places two quarters on the bar, one neatly stacked on top of the other.

Ms. Hanover, walks down the bar, and pours the man a glass of beer without asking.

He nods.

"How's it going, Hackensack Mack?" she asks, sliding over a plastic basket filled with pretzel sticks.

He slowly reaches for a stick.

I hate bums. I hate when I give them money, and I hate when I don't. I don't think Ms. Hanover really meant that.

I slide off the bar stool. "Good-bye, Teach."

"Yeah, scram," she says. "See you Monday, third period."

"Hey, aren't you finishing your drink?" asks Freddy.

"No. I'm finding Lavender."

Norman scoffs, and a nasty little sound comes out his nose, like a nose fart. "She's dead."

My cheeks redden, and I feel a quick spurt of anger. "Shut your dirty trap, old man!"

"Hey!" spouts Norman, standing up. "Let's have a little respect here!"

"Shut your dirty trap, old man, *please*," I say.

"Okay, that's better," he says, sitting back down.

I lean across the bar and whisper to Ms. Hanover, "I hate him." He's the type of guy who shits in people's shoes and pisses in pickle barrels.

"Don't hate," she says. "You become what you hate. Now, scram."

Chapter 24

NEW YORK CITY IS TEACHING me two huge lessons: ignore appearances and don't always believe what you think. That pot-smoking poet on Bleeker Street, that purple-headed guitarist, and pink-tutu girl, are probably liars. That fortune-teller, too. So is that English-French-speaking panhandler, Hackensack Mack, Funny Fred, and Norman. Even Ms. Hanover is a bit of a liar.

I start walking down the Bowery, checking my handsome reflection in plate glass windows as I pass. I resist the urge to flex my biceps.

"Hey, Matthew Watt!"

I turn around and see Funny Fred running toward me—his emerald green tie is fluttering in the wind. I start to run, but he grabs my elbow and slaps my back. I don't like when a strange man slaps my back.

"I told you," he says, "I know Popeye's favorite spot! C'mon, turn around—Broome's this way." In the daylight, his skin is grayer and his teeth yellower. This dude's giving me the heebie-jeebies, but I'm down here to find Lavender, and that's exactly what I'm gonna do.

He leads the way.

We continue walking down Bowery Street and hang a right on Kenmare. Finally, we stop in front of an alleyway. He looks left and right. "I don't understand," he says, placing his hands on his slender hips. "She's usually sitting right here."

"You sure?"

"Sure I'm sure." He sort of frowns, angry with me for questioning him. Then he says, "C'mon! I know another place."

He leads me up an ugly street full of liquor stores with dirty windows, a delicatessen with three clashing colors, a cheap motel, and a massage parlor. No Lavender.

"Well, it was worth a shot," he shrugs.

We stare at each other.

"Don't blame me if a starving mutt roams around scavenging for food." He fishes a Lucky Strike out of his pack, puts it between his lips, and lights up. "Let's not lose hope, kid," he says, inhaling deeply. His face is tough from the weather and deeply lined. He lets the cigarette smoke out through his nose, and it drifts in a cloud in front of his face. He stands there silently, studying me. I avoid his stare by looking up and down the street. I don't like being stared at, and his stare is weirding me out.

"Well," he finally says, "might as well try Barlow's room."

I glance up at him.

"Across the street from the Stone."

"Back where we started?"

He nods. "Yup, apartment 2C." He flicks cigarette ash onto the pavement. "I know where he hides his key."

The idea of breaking into Barlow's apartment doesn't sound too cool, plus I definitely don't wanna get caught inside alone with this freak. But I have no choice. I can't listen to my inner sissy and punk out. I have vowed to find Lavender.

Funny Fred, I notice, has slender manicured hands, narrow shoulders, and a long neck. Even though he's older and a foot taller, if I got stuck in an apartment with him alone, he'd be a can of corn. I happen to have a damn good left hook. That's a fact.

"All right," I say. "Let's go."

We start walking back toward the Blarney Stone. Halfway down the block I ask, "Why does Norman call you Funny Fred?"

He's too busy smoking his Lucky Strike to answer. At the corner, he takes a long drag and flicks the butt into the sewer. "Don't listen to that errant knave. He's got shit for brains."

"Nice way to talk about your friend," I say.

"Do I detect sarcasm?" he sniffs.

87

We stop at the corner of Elizabeth and Spring. Old winos are napping in the warm afternoon sun, and I smell puke and piss.

"Just call me, Fred. Okay? I'm not a loser, like my friend," he says, with his deep baritone voice. "I'm a painter, like my mother. But the lowlife environment here lures me. I'm attracted to human frailty — like a moth to a flame." He points to a bum. "Like him." A wino is pissing a nice yellow stream on a brick wall in broad daylight. Downstream is another panhandler picking through a trash can. They have no shame.

"Just look at all this human debris," he says, shaking his head. "It's terrible, but I delight in painting these damaged men. I capture the buried pain and anguish within their faces. William Burroughs does it with literature. I paint it."

We look at each other, and it's like I'm looking into a mirror. I see a guy choosing negativity — just like Mimi Breedlove had said about me.

What am I doing to myself? Day by day, inch by inch, I'm evolving into a bum. I'm a classic underachiever.

I should be playing baseball.

I look at Fred's tired gray face and then at the man fumbling with his penis.

I feel so ashamed

Fred grins. "Welcome to the Bowery!"

Chapter 25

FUNNY FRED AND I CONTINUE walking up Elizabeth Street, then curl back onto Prince, a thin treeless street. We look down dark alleys and under dirty stoops and call out Lavender's name, but the only animals we see are pigeons.

We look down Bowery Street and Rivington, two droopy streets. There's plenty of dog shit, but no Lavender.

"I hope she didn't run out into traffic again," says Funny Fred.

"Again?"

He nods. "Why you think her eye's sticking out? She was burying a bone in a pothole in the middle of the street. Car missed the pothole but hit her."

Whew! I knew Barlow didn't slug her.

It starts spitting rain, and my high-top Cons are getting wet. It seems like we're walking an awful long time accomplishing nothing.

Fred stops, leans against a phone booth, and stares at me. "It's been bothering me since I first met you. You remind me of someone… it's about the face." He shrugs and we continue walking.

He points to a brick building across the street. "There's CBGBs. Alotta new punk bands are playing there—The Ramones…Blondie." He puffs on a new Lucky Strike. "Once upon a time, the Bowery was nothing but flophouses and whisky joints, but now it's becoming gentrified. It doesn't look like it, but old apartments are being renovated. Evolution, I guess. Everything's gotta evolve."

I think of Sailor Barlow's evolution: world champion, painter, street bum.

My brother's evolution: student, drug addict, gone.

My father's evolution: father, song writer, missing.

My evolution: school president and Most Popular, athlete, depresso-narcissist.

Funny Fred shakes his head. "The Bowery's reinventing itself. Now it's celebrity lounges and million-dollar lofts. Fortunately, there's still enough quaint sleaziness."

Funny Fred points to another brick building. "Thar she blows! The Sunshine Hotel! The last flophouse left! Seventy-five men live there—each gets a small cubicle, cot, and locker. They share a communal bathroom. Rooms are four fifty a night. My friend Norman lives there."

"Really?"

"So did Benny."

"Sailor Barlow?"

He nods. "Until they threw him out."

"Why?"

Funny Fred stops and leans on a lamppost. He reaches into his back pocket and flips out another Lucky Strike, sticks it into his mouth, and lights up. He tilts back his head, takes a lungful of smoke, and lets it come out slowly through his nose. "Toxic fumes. Barlow polluted the whole fourth floor. Easels, paint cans, paint tubes in the sink, turpentine rags—guys were getting sick. So they kicked him out."

"Where'd he go?"

"Where we're headed."

We continue walking.

"Truth is, and I hate admitting it," he says, "the son of a bitch is a gifted painter—better than I'll ever be. But he became a recluse and paint addled his brain. Maybe he's punchy, but it's the paint poisoning that finally got him. I'm certain of that."

"What do you mean?"

"He got too passionate and painted himself sick. He married painting like a nun marries Christ."

I stand here thinking twisty thoughts and I feel a knot of pain growing inside my stomach, growing with each second.

"Benny escaped life and dove into art. Artists do that sometimes. A lot of the bums down here were once successful executives or family men, but when life got too tough, it's *Stop the world, I want to get off.*" He shakes his head. "You're too young to understand."

But I do understand—perfectly. I'm looking up at the dirty windows of the Sunshine and feel a miserable connection with the men wasting away inside. *Stop the world, I want to get off* is exactly how I feel.

Funny Fred looks at me for a long time. "Why you looking for Popeye anyway? I mean, what's in it for you?"

I bend down from the sharp pain stabbing my stomach. What have I gotten myself into? Why am I searching for a lost dog when it's me who's lost?

Norman's probably right—she's already dead.

Funny Fred eyes me. "You okay, kid?"

I'm sick. I realize I'm not searching for anything—I'm just running from everything. I'm a high school casualty destined for bumhood. I'm gonna puke right here and now.

"You look pale," he says. I wipe sweat from my forehead.

"Anyhow," he continues, "the poor old bastard did two things well—punch people and paint 'em. The last time I visited him, I open his door and Holy Christ! The room was a thick toxic cloud, and he was slumped in a chair, naked and unconscious. I thought he was dead…"

Naked and dead?

"…and then when I look around his apartment, I see unstrung masterpieces hanging on his fuckin' walls."

It feels like I'm being stabbed in my gut by everything—stolen paintings, dead Lavender, naked Barlow, and the ugly insights into myself. "Stomach…," I mumble, rubbing it.

Fred snorts and shrugs at the same time. "Sonny, those paintings're worth millions!"

"Paintings don't just disap—". Suddenly, puke gushes into my mouth and splashes onto the sidewalk and my shoes.

"Whoa!" gasps Fred, hopping back.

"Hey, let's get you cleaned up!" He points to a five-story walk-up, with black fire escapes zigzagging down the front. "That's my apartment over there."

We cross the street and he quickly pulls out a key from his hip pocket, inserts it into the lock, and say, "C'mon in." He holds the door open. "First, take off your shoes."

My Cons are wet with puke and a strange man is inviting me into his apartment. I guess it's my own damn fault, committing myself to save an injured dog.

"C'mon, I won't molest you," he smiles, waving me in.

Maybe he's a terrific liar, but he knows where Barlow hid his key, so I decide not to be a wimp. I'm gonna find Lavender--whatever it takes.

Chapter 26

I WALK TO THE OPEN door and stop.

"C'mon in!" He kills his cigarette with his shoe, holds the door wide open and motions me inside. "Let's relax with a cold brewski."

That's when I see the dog! "Lavender!" I jump off the steps and sprint down Kenmare. "Catch her!" I scream. "Catch her!"

I run to the corner, turn at Elderidge, and bump into a hardhat reinventing the Bowery. "Catch her! Catch her!" I yell.

"I kept running and running. Of course I didn't catch Lavender because, well, there *was* no Lavender."

Ralph Kramden, the bus driver, looks at me confused. "Whaddya mean?"

"Don't ya get it? I lied! I just wanted to get away from Funny Fred," I explain.

He's sitting on his bus at the 175th Street Port Authority bus terminal collecting fares from passengers going across the George Washington Bridge, back to New Jersey. "So, you didn't actually see her?"

"No. I just wanted to escape Funny Fred."

He grins. "Ah! Now I get it! That was genius!"

"Yeah, well, I never got my cold b-brewski."

He then turns back to his job, adjusting his mirror, making sure everyone is safely seated. He turns the key, and the engine begins to rumble. The bus pulls away from the curb onto the upper level of the bridge.

Ralph Kramden has the relaxed manner of someone confident in his ability to beat your butt or throw you off his bus if he has to. An empty coffee cup sits in a tray beside him, along with a folded copy of the *Daily News*. "So, you never found the dog, huh?" he asks.

"Nah. It's not possible. She's probably dead."

"Well, seek and ye shall find," he says, shifting gears and pulling into the left lane.

I look out the window at the Palisade Cliffs on my right, then down at the gray Hudson River flowing below. As usual, my brain's full of questions. Where is Lavender? Who stole Barlow's paintings? Did toxic paint screw up Barlow's brain? Were Barlow's paintings really worth millions? Was Barlow a genius or a monster?

I think of the famous painting of George Washington crossing a river, standing there in a small boat, all heroic and courageous, seeking victory from the Redcoats. Me, I'm crossing the Hudson River in a Greyhound bus seeking to rescue a damn dog with a wiener-sausage eye.

Lavender is becoming an obsession, and I'm okay with that. I wouldn't change it for the world.

Seek and ye shall find.

"Who was that cutie pie you skipped school with the other day?" asks the bus driver. "The one with the long black hair."

"Nobody." Ralph Kramden, who I keep running into, has a good memory.

"She's a very pretty nobody."

"Just a friend."

"Friend or *girl*friend?"

I'm silent.

He's a big, solid man with short reddish hair, and his MTA coat hangs on a hook behind him. Orange suspenders are strapped over his white short-sleeved shirt.

"I think you want her to be your girlfriend," he says. "Am I right?"

We're heading west, and the late afternoon sun is slanting in on us. He squints and lowers his sun visor. "Am I right?" he repeats, looking back at me.

PETER WOOD

I imagine Mimi Breedlove in her bedroom, sitting in front of a mirror, brushing her silky black hair that cascades onto her soft breasts. Just thinking of her gives me a massive boner.

"You love her?" he asks.

"No, I don't *love* her," I spit.

"No need for attitude," he says.

"No attitude."

He grins. "Yeah—you love her."

It's none of his damn business. But, sure, I do love her, even though she's a bit of a psycho. She's a pretty psycho who slam-dunked me just because I didn't ask her questions. The truth is I think I did ask her one—I think.

"A gorgeous girl like that, you can't just twiddle your thumbs, pal," he says. "You gotta make a serious play."

"I'm not a player," I say softly.

"What's that mean?"

"It means these past few years, I've lost my confidence. Maybe it's low blood sugar or schizophrenia or my brother's weak genes," I feel like saying, but don't.

"Show her you're genuine," he says.

"H-How?"

"Take her to a movie." He looks out his side-view mirror, turns on his right signal, and steers back into the right lane. "Buy her something," he says. "You know—candy or flowers."

"Cor-ny."

He shrugs. "You got a better idea?"

We sit quietly.

"How'd you end up here?" I ask.

"Being a bus driver?"

I nod.

"Why you ask?" he says.

I shrug. My question has more to do with me. Would I ever find a decent job and fit into society when I grew up? Or was I gonna become a bum.

"Me, being a bus driver," he says, looking over at me, shifting his eyes without moving his head. "I was lucky. My ex-wife's father knew somebody who knew somebody in the MTA. It's good to have connections."

95

But *connections* is what I'm afraid of. Connections is a dog leash. Connections is a punch in the face. Connections is scuzzy friends who piss in pickle barrels. Connections is pain.

"You like driving a bus?" I ask.

"Driving these double shifts pays the rent and keeps me outta trouble. And the bonus is I meet interesting people—like you."

"No need for attitude."

"No attitude."

We both grin.

He keeps driving straight into the sun and Fort Lee is coming up fast—so is that pretty Clairol woman on the billboard. She's still giving me her shit-eating grin.

The brakes screech and the bus slows down at the curb. "Yeah, she's a real cutie pie," says the bus driver. "Reminds me of my ex-wife—when she was younger, of course."

Mimi is, indeed, beautiful. And beautiful girls—especially smart ones—stir up a deep sense of inferiority within me. Maybe it's a glandular deficiency.

He cracks open the door. "Remember, buy her something nice—a token of your affection."

"Corny," I say, stepping off.

He looks down at me. "Kid, lemme ask you something: If you stand on the beach waiting to see what washes up, is that fishing?"

I have to think on that one.

He starts to close the door. "Invite me to your wedding!"

I run up the concrete stairs, two at a time. I hop onto the #84 Red & Tan—my connection back to Closter.

I don't know about a wedding, but I know exactly what this depresso-narcissist is gonna buy pretty Mimi Breedlove. And it isn't candy or flowers.

Chapter 27

A T LUNCHTIME, THE DELIVERY GUY is waiting for me at the high school entrance.

I grab his box, pay him, and quickly wrap it up in a black plastic garbage bag that Skippy, our janitor, gave me from his rolling cart. Then I pretty it up with three pink bows I bought last night at the Dollar Store. After yesterday's therapy session on the bus with Ralph Kramden, I'm actually looking forward to giving Mimi this "token of my affection."

Without tilting the box, I walk into the cafeteria. Whenever I enter this high school hellhole and see everyone smiling, I think I might not be as damaged as I think. I bet most of these smiles are phony. Kids are pretending happiness.

There are no accurate words to describe the hidden adolescent turmoil flowing through our cafeteria. That's a true fact. Everyone is secretly wrestling with teenagerness. They're thrashing around with tangled thoughts, think-twists, and youthlet egos. I wish there was some type of mental tool, like an emotional eyelid, to protect us from our own teenage crap.

It's tough hanging around my peers each day with our silent grudges and loud anger and murmuring resentments and penis problems and breast issues and self-esteem dramas and artificial happiness and anorexia and ghetto attitudes and wannabe-ghetto-attitudes and self-mutilation issues. I could go on.

I can handle only one person's dysfunction at a time — mine.

I walk to Mimi's usual lunch table in the middle of this emotional bloodbath called a high school cafeteria. Her table is oozing with prettiness—junior and senior princesses, all nines and tens. And they know it.

"W-Where's Mimi?" I ask.

"How should we know?" grins a blonde ten with big tortured hair and big tits. She's wearing a bulging Bay City Rollers t-shirt.

"Because she usually sits here."

"Yeah, well, no more," says a nine-point-nine eating a curly fry, deep-fried in cholesterol. She gulps it down with lukewarm milk, and I can hear her cute little arteries clogging. She has medium-sized tits.

"Why not?" I ask.

"Don't you know?" smirks a blonde nine-point-eight, wearing green platform shoes, a week's worth of mascara, and green eye shadow. Her pink tank top says: "Smart Blond." Pointed tits.

I stand here silent.

"Wow! He doesn't know!" says a blonde nine-point-six with long pink fingernails and Cleopatra hair. Braless.

They giggle.

They can giggle their pretty little hearts out for all I care. "What's in the trash bag?" asks the blonde ten, pointing.

"Something."

"For pretty Mimi?" She grins. It isn't a nice grin.

I nod.

"Whaddya know, a gift of love in a plastic trash bag!" laughs medium-sized tits. "Mimi will adore it!"

They all giggle ugly giggles. I'm probably interrupting their deep conversation about who's the cutest Monkee.

"So where's Mimi?"

"Check the psychiatrist's office," whispers big tits.

"Hey, M-M-Maryjane!" It's Buzz, sitting at our table. He's wearing his usual zit-colored Led Zeppelin T-shirt. Tommy and Little Gus sit with him.

I point to his two black eyes. "Nice eyes, tough guy," I grin. "Who punched you?"

"Yeah, well, what's in the bag, douchebag?" Buzz's thugness is so thick, you can cut it into squares and build a wall with it. If I hang around these shits any longer, I'll catch fleas or a brain virus.

"Sit down." He offers the seat next to him—a spot smeared with mayonnaise.

"See my fist, Broadnax? I'm gonna shove it right up your fat ass, except you'd probably enjoy it." It's a good line, and I normally would say it, but I'm done with their infantile crap.

I jog up and down the school hallways, careful not to tip Mimi's gift.

I run upstairs. I run downstairs.

This little gift comes from the bottom of my heart, and I can't wait to see the big smile on her pretty face when she opens it.

I check the psychiatrist's office.

Locked.

It's warm and sunny outside, so I check the football field behind the school.

I see her upon the top bleacher, sitting alone. She's wearing her white short-sleeved shirt decorated with pink and green stars and planets, puff blue shorts, and pink flip-flops. Her long bare legs are nice and tan.

I climb up the bleachers, step by step, holding her gift. Why is talking to a smart, beautiful girl always so damn scary? Stick out chest.

Flex muscles.

Smile.

Talk.

"Hi, Mimi. I brought you a..."

Something is wrong...

A brown baseball cap is pulled down over her forehead. Her head is cradled in her hands. She removes her cap and looks me smack in the eye. My knees buckle, and I almost drop her gift. She's bald. Not exactly bald, but her hair is chopped off. Her long black hair is spiking up like bristles on a hairbrush.

I stand there, holding the gift, staring at her brutal haircut.

"Do you think there's life after death?" she asks.

I'm tongue-tied. There seems to be something to say, but I don't know exactly what it is. My brain's exploding with crazy thoughts, like cancer and chemo and funeral parlors and coffins, but I say nothing. Instead, I put her gift down beside her and reach out to hold her hand.

She takes it.

"W-who's dying?" I almost ask, but don't. It ain't a nice question to ask.

Silence.

"What's in the bag?" she says.

"A gift."

"For *moi*?"

I nod.

She begins tearing up, so I pat her leg. It's probably the wrong move because she bursts into tears. She can't stop sobbing, so she jams her fist into her mouth to keep quiet.

"You want to be left alone?" I ask.

She shakes her head and wipes her eyes with the back of her hand.

"Is my makeup smudged?"

"You look beautiful," I say.

"I'm sorry for being such a crybaby," she says into her hands. Her fingernails, I notice, are still red raw, chewed to bits.

"You wanna t-talk?" I ask.

She glances up at me and smiles weakly. "You can't just come up here and not give me my gift."

I hand her the bag.

She plucks off the three pink bows, slowly unwraps the black plastic, and pulls out a flat box. "Pizza."

"Thin crust."

She reaches out and hugs me. I can feel her sad wet smile on my shoulder.

Chapter 28

MIMI BENDS DOWN TO SMELL her pizza, then looks up and smiles. "My God, I like you, Matt. I like you very much. In fact," she adds, "I think I like you more than you like yourself."

I blush, and the muscles in my stomach flutter. I know Mimi's new opinion of me is only temporary. She'll like me until she doesn't, then she'll slam the door again. Just like my mom did to my dad.

Mimi is doing a terrific job disguising whatever is bothering her, until a tear plops onto her pizza. She places the slice on her lap, blows her nose on a paper napkin, and then wipes her face on her arm.

It's June, the end of the school year, and all five-feet-eight inches of the depresso-narcissist has limped through eleventh grade. She's limping, too. Why?

"Someone told me in eighth grade you were class president and voted Most Popular, right?" she asks, wiping tears from her eyes. I shrug and hand her another napkin. She takes it.

"What happened?" she asks, blowing her nose.

I shrug again. I don't wanna think about my high school self-destruction, my dope-dealing brother, or my lost father. It's none of her business anyway.

We sit quiet.

"Matt, I need to tell you something."

Just then the bell rings ending lunch.

She quickly stands up, grabs her bag, and drags me down the bleachers, across the football field. She's heading toward the far corner, to a hole in the chain-link fence. She flashes me a smile and begins running as fast as she can. "I'll beat you!"

I trot behind her. Her brown baseball cap is bobbing up and down and her pea-green bag is swinging side to side. Her legs are nice and long. She is a cutie pie.

"Beat you!" she says, scrunching her body through the fence opening.

"I let you," I say, squeezing my massive shoulders through the jagged opening.

My hands are jammed inside my front jean pockets as she tugs my arm and drags me across Columbus Avenue into the coolness of the Demarest Nature Center. Her urgent tugging makes me nervous, like an invisible dog collar is wrapped around my neck. But I follow her where she wants me to go — away from school, into the woods.

I know exactly where we are headed.

The dirt trail is cool and soft, and birds are chirping in the trees. A frightened rabbit nibbling on a white bud of clover, scampers across the dirt path and hides under a bush. This nature trail is strictly off-limits to us underclassmen — it's senior territory where they explore nature by kissing, petting, and fucking each other.

If seniors caught us trespassing, we'd be dead.

No problem, I calmly inform myself. I'm very good with my hands.

Mimi's hands are clutching my arm above my elbow, yanking me deeper into the woods. "I need someone now," she says, "and that someone is you."

We walk quietly, not saying much. It's a perfect time to talk, but I have nothing to say, so I just shut up and listen to her pink flip-flops *flip flop* on the soft carpet of pine needles.

At least I'm connected to something, whispers that dog-guy in my mind.

After a few more frightened rabbits, a chipmunk, and a lot of trees with hearts carved into their trunks, we reach a huge boulder. Every student in school has heard rumors about this boulder — it's called The Hump for obvious reasons. We climb up on top of The Hump and she plunks down her bag. She sits.

"Nice, isn't it?" she says.

"Guess." I shrug.

"Ah, a man of many words."

It *is* nice, except for all the graffiti and beer cans.

The top of The Hump is smooth and flat like a bed. She pats the rock, signaling for me to sit beside her. I sit, and throw back my shoulders, the way dad had taught me in fourth grade.

She looks at me and hugs her knees to her chest. "You're lucky you're not popular anymore. My father says if you're popular and have too many friends, you become a follower."

I don't say anything. I'm slow with a new idea, and I need to let that one sink in.

She looks at me with a friendly grin. "He says people need only one friend, preferably a strong one."

I don't say anything.

Her shoulder gently nudges me. "Are you my strong friend?"

"I thought you h-had a boyfriend."

"*Had*," she says, without going into detail. Instead, she reaches up and ruffles my hair. "You bought me thin-crust pizza! That was so sweet!"

It's going good between us, but I don't get my hopes up. My batting average with Mimi isn't so hot. Our bus conversation started good but ended in disaster. I have the rare gift of screwing things up in the end.

Mimi lifts off her brown cap and instinctively shakes loose her long black hair, which, of course, isn't there. I guess she forgot. Then she gazes up into the tall apple tree stretching above us and studies it. I never noticed how cute her little ears are, or how long and beautiful her neck is. She is a magnificent female creature. Too bad the depresso-narcissist is gonna fuck it all up.

"I want to tell you something," she says, closing her eyes. "But you can't tell anyone."

I nod.

She opens her eyes and sighs. "When I moved here from Columbus, Ohio, all those pretty girls befriended me, but honestly, I'm sick of them. All they talk about is ironing their hair, pedicures, makeup, and the slutty tattoos they're planning to get next year. They're cheerleaders, for God's sake! I mean, there's nothing wrong with cheerleading, but let's face it, it's all about people staring at their skinny legs and pretty little boobies."

Mimi has skinny legs and pretty little boobies too, and I like staring at them. What's wrong with that?

Hugging her knees to her chest, she rests her left cheek on her knee, then looks over at me. "So, are you my strong friend?"

I feel a delicious stiffening in my pants. I nod.

She gets thinkative and looks back up into the apple tree. When Mimi concentrates, she concentrates.

"You're special," she finally says, looking back at me. "I sense it."

Mimi, if you knew the real me, you'd puke.

She gently bumps her shoulder against mine. "Deep down, you know you're special," she whispers.

I raise my eyebrows.

"Absolutely!" She smiles, slowly rubbing my left arm with her hand. "In fact, you remind me of someone."

Why is everyone saying that—Funny Fred, Big-Nosed Norman, and now Mimi?

She grins knowingly and looks back up into the tree.

The midday sun is streaming through the leaves, and the soft rumble of traffic from Columbus Avenue drifts into the woods. I can hear a distant murmuring, like the sound of someone drilling a hole into something hard, probably with a jackhammer.

"May I borrow a trillion dollars?" she asks.

I look at her. "Huh?...What for?"

"It's a secret."

"Can't have it then."

Suddenly, she looks dead serious. "Well, can I, at least, trust you with a secret?"

I nod.

"You won't tell anyone?"

I look at her small ears, her chopped hair, and her red finger tips, and nod.

"Pinky swear?" she says. We wrap pinkies and press thumbs.

She inhales and says, "My father's very sick. He has some horrible skin disease." She sways her knees back and forth. "Two months ago he returned from a Florida business trip, itching and scratching. He can't stop. These little bug-thingies are crawling under his skin. He tried treating it himself, but…" She closes her eyes and shakes her head. "He keeps scratching and scratching. And now these horrible red sores are spreading all over his body. It's gross."

"Lice?"

"We thought lice or bed bugs, but it's not that."

I keep silent.

"He's visited specialists, and they all say the same thing: *delusional parasitosis*. They think it's all in his mind."

I look at her red, raw fingertips and notice my thumb beginning to itch. I scratch it.

"We've fumigated our house, decontaminated our carpets, and sterilized our furniture. It's costing us a fortune, but these little bugs are still crawling inside his skin. I'm scared to death."

I notice my other hand beginning to itch. I scratch the back of it, the palm, and between my fingers and on the web.

She looks down at a tiny black ant crawling beside her leg and squishes it with her thumb.

"My dad isn't delusional. What's delusional is he's losing his job, and we might lose our house. We just moved here!"

She begins to tear up again. I feel awful for her, but I also feel another itch—on the back of my left arm, above the elbow, exactly where she had been tugging me into the woods. I scratch it.

"This morning he woke up with a red sore on his lip!"

She looks down at the rock and squishes another ant, and another, and another. "So now he's beginning to get disgusting sores all over his face. He's a salesman, damn it! Clients love my father, but how can they love him with big repulsive sores on his cheeks and lips?"

Suddenly my left arm begins itching like crazy. I scratch it.

"How can a doctor not see something's wrong? I'm a high school junior, and even I know it's not a figment of his imagination."

I keep scratching my arm and wonder when big repulsive sores will start breaking out on my lips. I don't wanna kiss Mimi anymore. "Is it contagious?" I ask, scratching.

I don't think she likes my question. She narrows her eyes, finds another ant, and mashes it with her fist. "Die! Die! Die!"

Chapter 29

MIMI STARES AT ME. "YOU want to know why I cut my hair, don't you?"

What I really want to know is if her father's skin-thing is contagious.

She scrunches up her face, rips off a pink flip-flop, and begins smashing more ants. Whap! Whap! Whap! "I cut it because…" She begins crying and squishing every ant in sight.

"Never mind," I say. "It's none of my business."

"No, I'll tell you." Whap! "It's because I love my father!"

Whap! Whap!

"I love him! So I found this shop, this small boutique, in Fort Lee…"

Whap! Whap! Whap!

"…that buys hair."

"Oh."

"I sold my hair and gave the money to my father."

I'm itching all over now. I scratch my scalp with both hands. I'm itchy like crazy.

Suddenly, she sees me scratching and her red-raw fingers fly up to her mouth. "Oh, no!" Her eyes widen in horror.

"It's contagious, isn't it?" I say, scratching.

She gasps. "I'm so sorry!"

I start panicking. Something wormy is crawling through my hair. "Do you feel bugs?" she asks.

"Hell, yeah!"

"In your scalp?"

"Yeah!"

"And in your skin—where I touched you?"

"Shit, yeah!"

She rolls onto her side laughing. After she catches her breath, she tries to touch my hand, but I snatch it away.

"I'm *so* sorry," she laughs. "It's a joke. I'm only kidding!"

I look at her laughing face and red claws and wouldn't kiss her if you paid me a million bucks. "You made that all up?"

"I shouldn't tease you. It's just that I'm so upset about my dad," she says, putting her pink flip-flop back on her foot. "Don't worry. It's not contagious."

"I feel bugs," I say, scratching.

That's when the little bitch sticks out her tongue, points to her head, and twirls her index finger around like I was crazy. She says my bugs are psychological, only a figment of my imagination. Everyone in her family felt bugs—her little brother, her, and her mother, but they were fine. Just fine.

"It's only psychological?" I say.

"Trust me. It's not contagious." She absently reaches up with her hand to run her fingers through her long hair, which, of course, still isn't there.

She watches me scratch my scalp and smiles. "It's so funny. It's like autosuggestion—like yawning. If I yawn, you'll yawn. Don't worry."

Trusting pretty girls isn't easy for me. "You're a bitch."

"Sorry," she says.

"So my lips aren't gonna break out in disgusting red sores?"

"Nooo!"

"You sure?" I ask, scratching.

"I'm *so* sure," she reassures. "It's not con-tag-i-ous! It can't be—everyone in my family is fine. Just fine."

The funny thing is, the itching suddenly stops.

"You're still a bitch."

"I'm sorry," she says, reaching for my hand and squeezing it.

I sit here, quiet, listening to a murmuring jackhammer in the distance. That's all I can think to do—listen to the faint sound of drilling. Somehow, it's soothing and I wiggle my toes inside my Cons, listening to the jackhammer jackhammering.

107

And the birds singing.

"So," I say, breaking the silence, "w-who do I remind you of?"

She squints and tilts her head. "You can't guess?"

"No."

"It's so obvious, dummy!" She grins.

I look at her.

"Me!" she says.

She smiles, and a catlike grin takes over her face. Somehow, her wide smile always sends a tickle into my belly. "You remind me of me."

Suddenly, she drapes her arm around my shoulder. I don't pull away. Not pulling away is a huge personal victory. We sit here quietly.

She suddenly asks, "Do you like yourself?"

That question is a curveball. I study a small black ant crawling on my thigh and whisk it away.

"You will." She nods. "Once you discover who you really are."

"I hate myself," I hear a soft voice say. It's my voice.

Silence.

"Sometimes," she says, "I hate myself too."

We both look up into the apple tree with its branches twisting in the bright blue sky. A few puffy clouds move along slowly. A soft breeze dances through the trees.

"My dad once told me any kid worth his salt hates himself at least once a day."

That's encouraging because I hate myself a million times a day. But suddenly, I don't know why, my eyes get damp. I have no idea where the tears come from. Mimi has this amazing gift of crawling into my head and cracking me open. She has a remarkable talent for yanking out my emotion. Maybe it's her prettiness, but I don't think so. I think it's just her special gift.

I trust her.

"Hey, cowboy, crying is nothing to be ashamed of," she whispers. Her voice is gentle, like a caress. "Crying is good."

"Not crying." I turn my head and start fiddling with a twig lying on The Hump.

"Crying is good," she repeats.

"Not crying."

"Crying in front of someone makes you closer to that person."

"Bullshit."

"Ah." She grins. "A man of many words."

I feel a squirt of anger spurt up inside me — just like last summer — during my mother's wedding to Jackass.

I look away from Mimi and spot a wet crack on the side of The Hump where water is trickling out, probably from an underground spring. I get jealous of The Hump because it can cry. It's so damn stupid getting jealous of a rock, but I am.

"How's Sailor Barlow?" asks Mimi, changing the subject.

My head is spinning with my mother's wedding, crying, and bugs.

"Sailor Barlow?" she repeats.

I dry my eyes with the back of my hand and tell her about Barlow's possible lead paint poisoning. I explain how I had told Wanda about the toxic paint, who then informed the doctors, who then adjusted Barlow's meds.

She smiles. "Matthew to the rescue!"

"Yeah." I shrug. "Hooray for me."

I look at her looking at me. Now would be a good time to open up and tell someone about my secret plan.

"You have a secret plan?" she says.

"To help The Champ."

"How?"

"I'm working on it."

"You're not going to tell me?"

"Not yet."

"When?"

"Soon."

She looks at me and tilts her head. "Tell me now."

"Well, it's crazy. But I'll tell ya this: It's a plan to have The Champ become The Champ again. To help him make a comeback. Probably won't work, but, hey, I'll give it a shot."

Her shoulder nudges mine. "I think I just found my new best friend."

I stay quiet.

"I think we're both on personal missions," she says. "Me with my dad and you with Sailor Barlow."

"My personal mission goes far beyond that, Mimi. It's to find a dog, and to find my dad — and to find myself." I don't say that; I just think it. But it's like she heard my thought.

"Matt, I know you better than you know yourself," she says. "You have black squirmy thoughts crawling inside your head, and they're much worse than silly little ants."

She's right.

"That's enough psychology for today." I stand up and yawn. "This has been an interesting conversation," I say, stretching my arms into the sky.

"Were you able to follow the hard parts?" She grins.

I turn my head and spit into the woods to hide myself—it's the most masculine response I can think of. Yeah, I had enough intimacy for one day.

I feel the warmth of sunshine slanting through the trees and onto my back. I throw a few quick punches, pretending I'm Sailor Barlow. She smiles up at me and holds out her arms for me to lift her up. Once she's standing, she dusts off the seat of her pants, stands on her tiptoes, wraps her arms around my neck, and plants a kiss on my lips.

Maybe I don't always screw things up in the end.

We slide off The Hump and quietly walk back onto the dirt path, hooking fingers along the way. Mimi suddenly stops and turns to face me. "You know who you are? You are *The Wonderful Matthew Watt*."

I look away and notice a rabbit smiling up at me.

"Say it," she orders. "Say it, Matthew. 'I am the…'"

I feel embarrassed, but I say it. "I am the…"

"Wonderful Matthew Watt. Say it!"

"Wonderful Matthew Watt."

"And don't you ever forget it," she whispers, squeezing my hand.

We start walking back on the path. "Wanna help me find a lost dog?" says The Wonderful Matthew Watt.

"Does it have fleas?"

"No. Just intestinal worms."

"Gross!" she cries.

"And a disgusting wiener-sausage eye."

"You're so *stoopid*," she says, yanking her hand away.

Chapter 30

SUMMER MEANS SWIMMING POOLS, ROLLERCOASTERS, and camping trips—but for the Wonderful Matthew Watt, it means summer school. That's because, let's face it, geometry sucks.

"Dinner!" calls my grandmother.

Halfway down the carpeted steps, I forget something and turn around and walk back up.

I open Daniel's bedroom door, turn on the lights, and grab his pool cue from the far corner. I turn around and see Daniel standing there chewing gum. I know he isn't really there, but, I swear, I can almost see him standing in front of his mirror, combing his duck-ass haircut with a cigarette wedged behind his ear.

"Where's mom?" he asks.

"Europe. A business trip."

"And Dad?"

I shrug.

Daniel shakes his head with disapproval and continues combing his greasy hair. He then reaches for his favorite high-roll collared shirt. I spot the tattoo on his arm: MOM & DAD written inside a red heart. Upscale Closter kids never got inked, but Daniel did. He was a sophomore, and his tattoo broke my mother's upscaled heart.

"Where are you, Daniel?" I say.

"Don't worry about me," he spits.

His black slacks are well-pressed, and his black pointy wingtips, with all those important perforations on the toes, are spit-shined. He's duded up for a nighttime of doo-wop under the streetlamps of Newark or Harlem.

"Hey, squirt!" he shouts. "Where you think you're going with my pool cue?"

Daniel always had a shitty attitude.

I shut the light and close the door.

My grandmother is sitting at the dinner table: white tablecloth, expensive crystal goblets, expensive china, expensive silverware, blue candles, and cloth napkins in gold napkin rings. "Who were you speaking with upstairs?"

"Daniel," I say. That shuts her up. She gives me a dirty look and retreats into the kitchen. I hear angry slamming of cupboards and pantry doors. I immediately feel guilty. Daniel is still a painful topic—a scab on everyone's heart. I'm such a dumb-ass.

When Gram returns, I'm relieved to see her smiling again— probably with the help of a shot of gin. Her smile is just in her lips.

"Sorry, Gram," I say.

She sits down and places a napkin on her lap. "How's summer school?" she asks, moving forward.

"Not bad."

"Learn anything today?"

"No." I cut into the meatloaf with the side of my fork.

"Nothing?"

"You know." I shrug, sticking my meat-loaf-and-mashed-potatoed fork into my mouth.

"You're a real chatterbox," she says. "How's the baseball team?"

"Gram, you ever heard of Jane Withers?" I say, cleverly changing the subject.

She looks up. "Strange you ask. I recently saw her on *Lost Stars*." She spoons brown gravy onto her mashed potatoes and passes the silver gravy boat to me. "She was the child star who played opposite Shirley Temple. Why?"

"Just wonderin.'"

After a long silence, she clears her throat. Her smile still isn't reaching past her lips. "You okay, Gram?"

"Matthew, I'm extremely disappointed in you."

"Why?"

"Don't play footsie with me, mister. You know damn well why."
Gram never curses, but *damn* flew out of her mouth like a rocket.

"I apologize, Gram."

She sits there glaring at me.

"What did I do?" I ask.

"Matthew, we need to have a little talk."

"Aren't we talking now?"

She sips her coffee and holds the cup in front of her face with both hands, just staring at me over the rim. Gram is a former Gibson Girl who has managed to hang onto her beauty in a honey-haired-rosy-red-cheeks type of way. But no one in our house gives her enough credit—including me. Last year, she drove all the way from Toledo, Ohio, to help us out with our *Daniel Nightmare.* My mother even persuaded her to stick around. This made it possible for my mother and Jackass to hop around Europe. Gram doesn't mind sleeping in the basement next to the washer, dryer, and slop-sink.

"You and I need to clear the air." She carefully sets down her cup and pushes her plate to one side. She blots her red lips with her napkin and leans forward.

"Is this gonna turn into one of those conversations?" I say.

"Matthew, I hope you're mature enough to understand that even though your mother isn't here, that doesn't mean she doesn't love you."

"Delicious mashed potatoes, Gram," I say, pushing gravy onto the meatloaf with my fork.

"I know you're angry with her."

I stick my fork in my mouth and draw it out clean. "What's in 'em—butter?"

"Parents are never as good as you want them to be," she says.

"Or margarine?"

She picks up her cloth napkin and throws it at me. "I'm going to slap you!"

"Pass the peas, please."

"Matthew! The truth is your mother has always felt that she didn't need to worry about you, like she did with Daniel. You're stronger—"

"And smarter."

"Well, that's what I used to think."

I look up from my plate.

"Ever since I've arrived here, you've been in some kind of emotional hibernation. You have a lot of bundled up anger. You need to let it go."

I grin. "You sure you want that?"

"Yes."

My face is calm, but my heart's jackhammering and my stomach's a tight knot. "Gram, you and I both know the truth — my former-prom-queen mother is now a plastic mannequin with a big sticky hairdo. She's immune to reality."

She nods her head.

"The truth is, she's never here, even when she is here."

She nods again.

That's when my anger explodes. "Lemme hammer it home, Gram! Where was she when Dan was going down the toilet? She and Jackass were too busy enjoying high society!" Yelling feels so fucking good.

Gram calmly picks up her coffee cup, and takes a sip. "Are you through?" She starts talking bullshit. Life is difficult, and at times it grabs us by our throats and…blah…blah…blah…life's unfair…we can't let it drag us down…blah…blah…blah.

She reaches out to touch my hand. I pull back.

"Dear, these past two years have been difficult for your mother…the divorce…Daniel's death. But she's slowly recovering and I'm proud of her. I've never known her to be as happy as she's been since marrying Jack."

"Proud of her?"

"Her resilience."

I look down at my peas.

"Matthew, be compassionate." She sighs, and continues, "Now, about your father."

"What about him?"

"Your father's a wonderful musician, I really mean that, but we both know he has a problem."

"Yeah, he drinks."

She pauses and adds, "Yes. He's made some poor decisions. And sometimes a wife, well, outgrows the very thing she used to love."

I've heard enough. I stand up to leave but she grabs my arm. "Sit down, mister! We're not finished!"

I point to the wall clock. "But my friends at the library —"

"Sit down! Your asinine friends can wait!" she spits.

"Gram, I got a test tomorrow! I gotta study!"

"Sit down!"

I sit.

"Your brother got himself expelled from school because of drugs," she snarls. "Is that going to happen to you, too?"

"No."

"You say that now, but you're heading down the same road, buster! How many times were you suspended this year for fighting? How many subjects you fail? How many days you skip? When I look at you, I'm seeing your goddamn brother!"

"Join the gang—so does everyone else in school."

She tilts her head. "Are you using drugs?"

"What?"

"You deaf? Are you using drugs?"

"No!"

"Why then are you skipping school?" she yells.

I can't tell her about New York City, or the Champ, or my secret plan—she'd explode even more.

"Matthew, I'm missing one hundred and fifty dollars from my purse. Did you steal it?"

I feel a splinter of shame rip into my brain. I look past her face, over her shoulder at Jackass's expensive Tiffany lamp.

She bangs the table with both fists, the plates jump. "I knew it! Why are you stealing my money? You've been sneaking into my bedroom and dipping your little fingers into my purse! Why?"

"I was going to pay you back."

"Damn right you are!" She laughs, but her laugh has no humor in it. "Ever since your parents left for Europe, you've taken complete advantage of me! You wake up when you want! Eat when you want! Go to the library when you want! And your bedroom is a pigsty!"

I'm guilty of everything she says.

"Are you buying drugs?"

"No!"

"Stop lying to me!" She grabs a fork, leans across the table, and points it at my head. "Are you?"

"No!" I shout.

"What do you do with my money?" she screams. "You're buying drugs!"

I sit silent, looking at the angry fork pointing at my nose. "Gram, please don't worry."

"Don't worry?"

"Stealing is wrong, I know, but I have a plan, and it's a good plan."

"A good plan?" she erupts.

"I'm helping someone."

"Who are you, Robin-fucking-Hood?"

Bus and subway fare, roses, pizza, and a secret plan all cost money.

"This is why you skip school and rob me? Because you're helping someone?"

I don't say anything.

"What's this plan of yours? Tell me!"

"I can't," I say. "Not yet."

She leans back in her chair and looks sick to her stomach. "Matthew, you're going to end up just like your brother."

"You mean dead—lying on a Burger King floor next to a toilet bowl dead—with a needle stuck in my arm?"

I stand up and walk away.

"And a loaded gun," she yells at my back. "Don't forget about the goddamn gun!"

Chapter 31

A FTER WASHING THE DISHES AND apologizing a few million times, I tell Gram I'm walking to the library to study for tomorrow's geometry test, which, of course, is a big, fat lie because there is no test. I'm meeting Mimi Breedlove at the pool hall.

My brother's Balabushka is safely tucked under my arm. He's still inside my head as I walk down Closter Dock Road. His naked body is still lying on the bathroom floor, the syringe is still sticking in his arm, and the loaded handgun is still on the floor by his head. Daniel found his escape — heroin.

There but for the grace of God go I.

I look down at my shadow walking alongside me. *"I see a dark shadow falling over you,"* whispers the gypsy. I quickly raise my head and lookup for all the good stuff, like Mimi told me. I touch a green leaf hanging from a thin sapling. The streetlights hum softly overhead and moths flutter in the arc of the light.

It's the beginning of August, the moon is above, and flower blossoms are giving off a light scent. I'm going on my first official date with beauteous Mimi Breedlove.

I walk past Moritz's Funeral Home wondering what's the best way to date a pretty girl. Last week, Daniel's greaser friends, who he shot pool with for money, were bullshitting in the Taaz pool hall on this exact topic, and they came up with five plausible options:

Option #1: Never treat a pretty girl special. Don't act awestruck by her looks and don't gush out compliments.

Option #2: Tease a pretty girl. Pretty girls can smell fear and insecurity in a boy, so be cool. Boyish charm works.

Option #3: Always keep a pretty girl off balance and guessing. That'll make her want to spend time with you. Just don't let your guard down and go wimpy on her. The very second she thinks she's in control, it's over.

Option #4: Never compliment a pretty girl. Never put her on a pedestal, where she usually sits with other guys. If you do, give her a small compliment, then follow up with something nasty.

Option #5: Run hot and cold with a pretty girl. If you haven't gone out with her yet, be extremely friendly, and follow up with a period of indifference. Or date her a few times, then drop her cold (with every intention of starting back up again). She'll be stunned.

I am leaning toward #3, as I begin shooting pool at my favorite green-felt pool table in the back right corner. But after waiting an hour for Mimi to arrive, I switch to option #4.

The Cousin Brucie Show is playing The Beatles, The Rolling Stones, and Beach Boys on the overhead speakers. My dad called this pop music poop music. His pop music was Pat Boone, Bobby Vinton, and Connie Francis, old fifties stuff. Dad didn't write poop music, even though it was flying out of every music store in America.

Maybe Dad couldn't write poop music.

So money got tight, and my mother divorced him.

So dad left town. Pop!...Poop!...Poof!

Now I'm stuck living with Jackass and his smelly pipe.

I grip my brother's Balabushka and slam the cue ball. It skips off the table and rolls away like everything else in my fucking life — my father, mother, brother, friends.

I glance over at the door for the zillionth time.

No Mimi.

"Up on the Roof" is playing.

My dad once told me a story about a scruffy poop writer who hung out at The Brill Building in New York. Dad said, "She pounded the pavement day and night, and I wished her luck, but doubted she'd ever find it." Well, that scruffy poop writer was young Carole King, and I was listening to her sing about when the world gets her down and when people are too much for her to face.

Mimi skips in, chewing on a wad of Bazooka, judging from the smell. "Sorry I'm late." She smiles.

I smack the two ball into the side pocket.

"You angry with me?" she asks.

"No."

"Are too."

"Am not."

"Are too," she says. "You hit that blue ball like you wanted to hit me."

I drill the yellow-striped nine into the corner pocket.

"Ouch!" she says.

She hops onto the stool next to the table. "Well, Mr. Grouchy, I'm happy."

"Good for you."

"Don't you wanna know why I'm happy?"

"Why?"

"Well, I just got back from the dermatologist's office, and we have very good news!"

I look up from the table.

"And I'll share it with you—if you stop frowning," she says, working the gum in her mouth.

I slam the fourteen ball into the side pocket and smile for her.

"That's not a smile."

"Is."

"That's a fake smile, but fine. Well anyway, the mystery's finally solved!"

"Mystery?"

"We discovered what's hurting my dad! Morgellons Disease. It's very rare; only one thousand cases have ever been reported. The symptoms are crawling, biting, and stinging sensations; finding fibers on or under the skin, and persistent skin lesions."

"Never heard of it."

"That's just it! Nobody has! But Joni Mitchell, you know—'Yellow Taxi'—has it too! She says blue, black, and red fibers stick out of her skin like mushrooms after a rainstorm. The fibers can't be forensically identified as animal, vegetable, or mineral."

"Yuck!" Yuck is the best I can come up with.

"This disease is like a slow, unpredictable killer," she says. "It's a terrorist disease that can blow up one of your internal organs, leaving you in bed for a year. That's what the literature says."

"That's your good news?"

"Well, at least we know why my father's sick. And we think we know how to cure it."

"How?"

She smiles. "Bleach!"

"Bleach?"

"Yup! Bleach!"

She combs her short hair with her red fingers tips and grunts. "You don't wanna know the alternative remedies — trust me, you don't wanna know."

I try a tricky eight-ball–one-ball combo into the corner pocket, but miss. I wish there was a simple remedy, like bleach, to disinfect my polluted self-esteem.

"Stop frowning, Matthew! You look like a prune."

"I'm not a prune."

"Well, your face looks like one."

I stop frowning and smile. I don't want my face to look like a prune.

"Much better!" she says. "I love when you smile. You become so… Yves Saint-Laurent-ish."

I smile wider.

"You're The Wonderful Matthew Watt, remember?" she says.

How can I forget? I put down my brother's stick, take her in my arms, and hug her. I feel bad for being so angry. "I hope the bleach works," says The Wonderful Matthew Watt. "Mimi, I'm going into New York Saturday to search for Lavender again. Still wanna come?"

"Of course I do!" she purrs, melting into me. "I'll even bring my dog whistle."

That night I'm lying in bed gazing out the window at the stars above. I read somewhere that Eskimos believe stars are holes in the sky where dead people can peek through at you. It's supposed to be comforting, but I think it's creepy, like being spied upon. *Daniel, I'm sorry I took your Balabushka tonight.*

I just can't sleep. So I close my eyes and begin thinking about Mimi's warm hug, and then a young Carole King finding success. I begin singing quietly about how on the roof it's peaceful as can be, how the world can't get to you.

Before drifting off, I come up a sixth option for dating a pretty girl.

Option #6: Dating a pretty girl like Mimi is exactly the same way you'd date any girl. Be honest. Be interested in her interests. Focus on her words, not her looks. Courtesy and respect are essential. And don't forget to look up and smile!

Goodnight, Mimi. Sweet dreams

Goodnight Sailor Barlow. I'm gonna find Lavender for you.

Goodnight, Dad… Wherever you are.

Rest in peace, Daniel.

Chapter 32

I'M SITTING AT MY DESK in my bedroom, figuring out the area of a trapezoid. On the radio, the Yanks are beating the Indians on a Bobby Murcer homerun. I close my geometry and pick up a letter that arrived today from Berlin, Germany. It's written on hotel stationery. Folded inside is a postcard of the Brandenburg Gate. I guess she thinks she's educating me with this shit.

> *Dear Matthew,*
>
> *You failed math? I'm so disappointed in you! We go away and you fall apart. What's happening to you? Gram also tells me you're spending too much time away from home. Are you playing baseball all this time? She also tells me she's missing money from her purse. Is that true? I'm shocked! Jack and I will sit down with you and have a serious discussion about your future upon our return. Make certain you pull your wake around the house — do the dishes, mow the lawn, and weed the flower deads outside.*
>
> *With deep concern,*
> *Mother*

"Hey, Mom, you just made two more Freudian slips. Did you mean *weight* and *beds*? Just admit it — I'm a painful reminder of my deadbeat father and dead brother." I open my desk drawer, throw the postcard inside, and close it.

Chapter 33

I STUFF A FEW TASTY dog biscuits in my hip pocket and sling my Kodak Instamatic around my neck. Mimi brings a dog whistle and a dog leash. We're going on our second date — to rescue the Champ's injured dog.

Our first problem is we find plenty of dog shit, but no dog.

The second problem is, by early afternoon, we're dead tired.

We've walked every inch of the Bowery a million times. Up Spring Street, down Kenmare, up Delancey, down Rivington, up Grand, down Chrystie. And every inch of Broome Street.

Mimi blows her dog whistle at every dirty dumpster and stinky garbage can. Dogs bark, howl, and jump on us. But not one is Lavender.

There are moments of hope while searching alleyways in nearby Little Italy or sniffing out dark nooks and crannies, but these moments are short-lived. We ask cops, hardhats, shop owners, and hotdog and pretzel vendors. We walk into grocery stores and pizzerias asking men and women behind counters, "You see a dog with a wiener-sausage eye?"

By two o'clock, Mimi's back is killing her and my feet are aching. Still, we keep searching. This is insane. But I'd still rather be here with pretty Mimi than playing left field.

And I discover a few interesting things about dog searching: When dog searching, I'm not sucked up into myself too much. Plus, dog searching teaches patience. I can do patience, but after four fucking hours, I'm not a huge fan of it.

Dog searching is also romantic, especially when I accidentally-on-purpose brush my hand against Mimi's. All morning, walking beside her, I feel special, even a bit mushy. But the funny thing is, when I glance over at her pretty face—her big brown eyes, high cheekbones, and wide mouth—I realize I'm looking past her face into her. She's beautiful inside.

After four hours, we cross Canal Street and enter Chinatown with all its loud clashing neon and dizzy foreign symbols. At Division Street we sit down under a statue of Confucius. Poor guy's covered with pigeon shit. Flying overhead are hungry pigeons and seagulls yelling at the humans below to throw them something.

Mimi places her hands on her waist, twists her back, and I hear a series of cracks. "Ahh!" she says. Then she reaches into her bell-bottom's front pocket, pulls out her dog whistle, puts it between her lips, and blows. Instantly, the pigeons and seagulls flap away. "See?" She grins. "We don't hear a thing, but they do."

"So?"

"So, dummy, don't you see? Just because we don't *see* Lavender, doesn't mean someone else isn't. She didn't just disappear into thin air." She pats my shoulder. "We'll find her. Just believe."

Thin teenage logic. But I go with it.

We limp down Pell Street, a curvy cobblestone lane, and a light breeze kicks up the city grit. "Lavender!" she calls. "Come to mama!"

In my mind, I watch us hobbling along, two crazy kids from Closter, New Jersey. It's a major miracle if we actually do find the damn dog.

The camera strapped around my neck's getting heavier.

We walk past Dim Sum Go Go, Hing Wah Noodles, and Sichuan Palace and finally settle on Hong Kong River. We walk in and sit at a wobbly table next to a huge fish tank filled with pretty orange and white fish with puckered lips and long billowy tails. On the right wall is a ginormous glossy mural of Hong Kong. Chinesey music, with plucked instruments, flutes, assorted cymbals and gongs is tinkling in the background.

Mimi rolls her sore neck and stretches her back again. Then she brushes back her hair, which she keeps forgetting isn't there.

An old Chinese hunchbacked waiter with straight black hair and crooked teeth hands us menus.

"*Xie-Xie*." I smile.

He stares at me and walks away.

"You know, finding Lavender," she says, "is extremely important for Mr. Barlow. There's no greater therapy than the love of a dog. I learned that in Miss Ifill's health class."

I don't wanna be reminded of school. I'm sick of books, and I'm not doing so good in summer school, either. My GPA is basement level.

"People need to be needed," she continues, placing her white napkin politely on her lap. "People need to touch and be touched. A dog does that."

"You're beautiful. And you say amazing things," I wanna say, but don't. Instead, I fidget with my white plastic chopsticks.

She closes her menu and leans forward. "Do you know what else dogs do? They love unconditionally. And they eliminate the language barrier. For a lonely man like Mr. Barlow, Lavender's an antidote to depression. Lavender is his family."

"Wow," I say. "I wish I said that."

"You wish you could," she grins.

I look at her. Sometimes she's a real smartass.

"Petting a loyal loving dog is better than taking some stupid pill," she adds.

I wish I said that too. But I'm the dumb one sitting at this table, the idiot attending summer school. Ms. Hanover is right—I'm a classic underachiever who will, most likely, repeat eleventh grade.

"What if Lavender is already chopped up into an eggroll?" I say.

Mimi frowns. "That's disgusting!" She pulls out her dog whistle and blows, and the fish inside the tank dart and splash. "See?" She smiles. "Human contacts fish! We'll find her. Just believe."

Our hunchback waiter walks over and takes our order.

"Egg drop soup, spring roll, and ginger ale, please," says Mimi, politely.

"Wonton soup, egg roll, and a Coke. *Xie-Xie.*" I smile.

He's so impressed by my Chinese mastery that he glances down at me. "Your Chinese sucks," he says. Then he walks away.

"So, Mr. Negativity," says Mimi leaning forward again, "what's your favorite memory?"

Her question is a curveball, a brush-back pitch. I squirm in my seat. "That's pretty random."

"It's called an adult conversation," she says. "Ever hear of it?"

Our waiter returns, placing a tall glass of ginger ale and a paper straw in front of Mimi and a Coke and straw in front of me.

"I gotta lot of favorite memories."

"Give me one." She drops the straw into her ginger ale, takes a tiny sip, and looks at me.

"Well…" I tell her about pitching a shutout for the Chicago White Sox in Little League when I was twelve. Then I tell her about my brown leather baseball glove and my baggy uniform and the home run I hit over the left field fence. I tell her about my utter confidence that day, with my father sitting in the stands watching me. I can still see his wavy brown hair, white shirt, blue striped tie, and proud smile.

Our nasty hunchback returns with our soup.

Mimi takes a sip of her egg drop and shoots me a look without saying anything. I know she's sizing me up. That's okay. I'm used to that. People never know what to make of me, so they ask questions until they think they figured me out.

She reaches across the table, picks out a few fried noodles from a bowl, and sprinkles them into her soup.

The waiter brings our entrées—a slim spring roll and a fat brown egg roll. He sets them down on the table and doesn't smile once. Mimi carefully spoons a small amount of orange sauce on her spring roll and takes a nibble. Her self-control is awe-inspiring.

"That's it?" she says. "A baseball game?" I shrug.

"Okay, I'll give you a memory—about my dad." Her memory is last night's medical update. With a magnifying glass, she and her mother discovered tiny black and blue hairs, or fibers, growing out of an open sore on his back. Her mother plucked them out, one by one, with tweezers and put them in an empty mayonnaise jar to show the dermatologist.

Suddenly, I feel jumpy. We're talking parents, and when kids talk parents, they usually end up bitching, blaming, crying, or cursing. My way of dealing with parents is to forget them. *Mom* and *Dad* are foreign words in my mouth. That's the truth.

I look at the fish trapped in the tank and sip Coke.

"How about your parents?" she asks.

"Let's talk about something else."

She narrows her eyes. "Why?"

This is a perfect time to squat under the white tablecloth and adjust our wobbly table. I bend down and wedge two sugar packets beneath one of the feet. I wish my wobbly brain could be fixed as easily — just wedge a little packet of sugar in my left ear and I'd be fine.

"Hello?" she says, looking at me from across the table when I return. "Your parents?"

I break into a cold sweat. I hate when that happens. Doesn't she get it? I don't do parents. Some people don't do meat or religion — I don't do parents. I gave up on parents a long time ago. I'm a parental atheist.

I look up at Hong Kong at night and crunch ice with my teeth. "Parents?"

"Don't you ever say 'Thank you' or 'I love you' to them?" she asks.

I keep crunching, studying the night lights of dark Hong Kong. We sit for a long time, listening to me crunch ice. "Why all these bullshit questions?"

"Oh, never mind," she says, throwing her napkin on the table. "Go hide under the table again. Get the check, stupid."

She stands up and stomps to the bathroom. When she returns, she gives me the dreaded silent treatment, standing beside the table, hands on hips, waiting for me to pay.

"My father is a composer," I say.

She sits down. "You mean a songwriter?"

I nod. "He's a tall man with a back I always saw hunched over the piano."

"Would I know any of his songs?"

"No, but your parents might." Suddenly I go silent. How can I explain to perfect Mimi that my father, like Barlow's injured dog, has vanished?

"Your father sounds like a gifted man. What happened to you?"

I set my glass back on the table and look at her. "Mimi, please don't get nasty with me. And don't call me *dumb* or *stupid* anymore."

She grins. "Okay…dummy."

"Why do you do that?"

She shrugs. "Sarcasm is one of my many talents. I'll be good from now on. I promise."

I take a gulp of Coke, and set down the glass. "Okay. Let me explain my father." It's amazing that I've managed to keep this secret for so long. "He's good at writing songs, but he has a problem…He's alcoholic."

Her mouth drops open, but doesn't say anything.

"No one knows where he is."

"Gosh," she says softly, "I'm sorry, Matt."

"Yeah, well." Now is probably when I'll hear the door slam.

"When was the last time you saw him?"

I shift in my seat. "Two years ago."

"This is the first time you ever spoke to me about your family," she says.

For some dumb reason I feel like crying, but I'm a tough guy and tough guys don't cry.

I've missed my father every single second of every single day. I wish I could buy a father whistle. I'd blow it on every street corner in New York City.

People don't just disappear into thin air.

Just dogs.

Chapter 34

AFTER LUNCH, MIMI AND I walk back onto Pell Street. It's partly sunny, and the seagulls are still up in the sky quarrelling with each other about whatever. Street vendors on Canal Street are hawking knockoff cassettes, fake Rolexes, phony designer purses, and replica Adidas sneakers—all lies.

The sun slips behind the buildings as we cross Canal, walk through Little Italy, and enter the Bowery. I notice men and women stealing quick glances at Mimi's pretty face as they pass. Walking with her is just like that—she's achingly beautiful.

The Bowery is noisy with machinery. Hardhats are tearing down old stuff and replacing it with new stuff, just like Funny Fred had said. Loud demolition projects, noisy construction jobs, and sandblasting is kicking up dust everywhere. The air is dizzy with redevelopment, and it's getting into everyone's hair and eyes.

Brick by brick, the area is busy reinventing itself with concrete mixers, tall metal cranes, and ear-splitting jackhammers. Young people with clean shaves and fresh perfumes are walking well-groomed poodles past winos lying on the warm asphalt streets. It's a weird mix: the rich and the poor; the young and the old.

Mimi and I are a weird mix too—an eternal optimist and a profound pessimist.

"So," she says, "tell me more about your secret plan."

"Ah…Still working on it."

"You said that last time."

"It's still in the planning stage."

She sighs and catches a hardhat glimpsing at her. "I wish you'd just tell me what it is."

"I wish I could, but I'm..."

"Yeah, I know, still working on it."

Hackensack Mack, the Champ's three-fingered roommate, is sitting in front of Barlow's run-down brownstone. He's sitting on the sidewalk, like before, propped against the red-brick wall, with another piece of ripped canvas cushioning his butt. I wonder if Mack knows his days are numbered. Very soon his building is gonna be gutted and he'll be relocated into a halfway house in Staten Island or Brooklyn.

"Hi, Hackensack Mack," I say, smiling.

He looks up.

I'm expecting another violent coughing fit, but he just sits there, wheezing.

"Starving," he gasps. Then he reaches out with his three-fingered claw.

I drop a quarter into it.

"God bless you," he pants.

His brown scab is healing, but his red eyes are still cloudy and his sunken cheeks have hit bottom. No way could this pathetic panhandler have stolen the Champ's paintings. But I ask anyway. "Where are Benny Barlow's paintings?"

He looks confused.

"Have you seen the Champ's paintings? How about Popeye?"

"Dog?"

"Yes! Mr. Barlow's dog."

He thinks long and hard. "I think...," he says.

"Where?"

He looks up into the dusty sky.

Brain silence. Confusion.

"Where?" I repeat. I hand him a dollar bill.

He pockets it.

"Is anyone taking care of Lavender?"

"Takin' care o' who?"

I kneel down beside him and slowly repeat myself. "Popeye... Lavender. Where is Mr. Barlow's dog? Where are his paintings?"

He thinks long and hard.

Brain silence.

"Starving," he wheezes. He hocks up a piece of yellow phlegm and spits.

Hackensack Mack is severely brain damaged, probably from huffing paint fumes and toxic air. He isn't going to be much help. But we came this far, I'm not gonna give up now. Lavender needs us, and I'm gonna find her if it kills me. If I flunk summer school and repeat junior year, I'll do it in a heartbeat.

I tell Mimi about the hidden key, hidden somewhere around Barlow's door. She looks up at the brownstone and grins.

We open the black metal door and peek inside. It's dark and stinks of piss and paint fumes. The walls are dingy green, and there's no light bulb in the socket above.

We step inside.

I gulp back fear as we slowly enter the dark hallway. I've been a wuss far too long, comfort-zoning my entire high school career, and it's gotta stop. I'm a hard rock. All I need to do is rebuild the courage-muscle in my brain.

I hate to admit it, but it's a huge comfort when Mimi grabs my hand and holds on tight as we walk up the narrow stairwell towards Barlow's apartment—2C.

On the second floor, behind a closed door, someone is coughing hard. Behind another closed door, we hear a man growling incoherent words while banging—his head?—against the wall. He sounds awfully angry. Is this where Wanda's head-banging boarder babies end up? We keep climbing up the stairs until I step on an empty liquor bottle. This is a dark insane place where weird is happening. We reach the second-floor landing and freeze.

Down the hall, on the left, we hear a barking dog.

Chapter 35

THE FLOOR AROUND 2C IS splattered with paint.

I knock softly.

Silence.

I turn the knob.

Locked.

I squat down and run my fingers along a jagged crack where the plaster wall and wooden floor are supposed to meet. No key. I pry loose a warped floorboard and feel beneath it. No key. Mimi is standing on her tiptoes inspecting the broken plaster around the door. No key.

Suddenly, across the dark hallway, a door creaks open. An old hatchet-faced woman with loud red lipstick and pink rouged cheeks steps out. At her side is a huge German shepherd. "Breaking in, eh?"

I tell her we're looking for Barlow's dog.

"Liars," she hisses. "World's full of liars!" Her nasty dog snarls and tugs at its leash. She pulls it back with her knobby little hands. "If I let this dog go, he'll tear out your throats."

"We're not thieves," says Mimi, holding out her arms.

"Are, too!" she says, grinning and frowning at the same time—heck of a neat trick. "I'm calling the cops."

"Madam," says Mimi quickly, "we're volunteers with the local ASPCA. We're told an injured dog lives here, a dog needing immediate medical attention. Have you seen a dog with a severe eye injury?"

The woman hesitates. "The ASPCA? Show me identification. A badge or somethin'."

Mimi smiles and shakes her head. "We're merely volunteers, ma'am. Unfortunately, they don't issue us badges. But we are animal lovers, like yourself, and are very concerned about the welfare of this sick dog."

"How do I know you ain't just tryin' to steal paintings?"

"The dog's name is Lavender," I say, getting off my knees.

She laughs. "Ya mean Popeye?"

I nod.

"How do I know you ain't lyin'?" she says, tilting her head.

I show her my camera. "For medical and documentary purposes," I say.

"Well…if you're stealin' paintings, you're too late. They're all gone. Everybody's looked a million times already. Been Grand Central Station that room. Poor horse puncher. People would rob the gold fillings outta his filthy mouth if they could."

Who took them? Funny Fred? Norman? Hackensack Mack?

Her dog is still growling and tugging at its leash.

"Henrietta here needs to go potty," she says, putting her hand on the stair railing. "I'm tellin' ya, there ain't nothing left in that room 'cept dog shit. Maybe you can sell the dog shit. Barlow's key, by the way, is taped to the bottom of the door."

She and Henrietta hobble down the dark stairwell and exit the front door.

I squat down and run a finger along the bottom edge of the door. I feel something and pull it out. A silver key! I stand up, stick it into the lock, and turn the knob. The door opens.

Thick cloud-fumes of paint and turpentine gush into the hallway — the same crappy air Barlow had been breathing since who knows when.

"Hello?" I call, holding my nose.

No answer.

I flick on the light and open a window.

The room is empty, but full of a stink. Cigarette butts, dead cockroaches, empty paint tubes, liquor bottles, and dog crap are everywhere. A large wooden table stands in the middle of the room, and a bare mattress lays in the far corner. No sheets. No chairs. No lamp. No rugs. No cabinets. No clothes. No TV. No paintings. No dog.

Only stench and dog shit.

Barlow's kitchen is on the windowsill — a hotplate.

I shake my head and grimace. This is so damn tragic. This pigsty is the home of a former world champion. A total disgrace.

"Matt! Come here!" calls Mimi from the bathroom. Her voice is trembling.

I look in, and what I see is solid and mean, like a slap across my face. A dog with short yellow fur and mismatched ears is lying on its belly next to the toilet bowl. Lavender.

She's dead.

I crouch down and feel her body. She's still warm, and the drool around her snout is still wet. I touch the piss on the floor around her legs. Warm.

"We'd better leave," says Mimi.

I quickly turn Lavender onto her back and begin pumping her chest.

Mimi gasps. "What're you doing?"

"What does it look like I'm doing?" I scream.

"She's dead."

"Call an ambulance!" I yell as tears stream down my face. There's still a chance. My hands begin shaking as I pump. My mind is a mixed-up mess, and Mimi probably thinks I'm going mental, and maybe I am, but it makes me sick to my stomach to think Lavender died just a few seconds before we arrived. My guilty conscience starts screaming — *If only you weren't so weak and selfish and hadn't stopped to eat a damn egg roll, you could have saved her!*

"Call an ambulance!" I scream. Then I bend closer, pinch her nostrils shut, open her jaws, and stick my lips over her mouth. I begin blowing air down her throat and into her lungs. I can smell her stomach, and it's pretty damn disgusting, but I keep blowing hard, pumping her chest with both hands until I think I'm going to pass out.

"Wass this?" says a voice.

I look up and see Hackensack Mack.

"You son of a bitch!" I yell.

"Wha?"

"You murdered her!"

"Matt!" says Mimi.

I go back to Lavender, pumping, and blowing fresh air into her lungs, but I know it's no good.

"Good riddance," wheezes Mack. "Mangy mutt."

134

I look up at him, and then back down at Lavender. The tears are coming from a deep place within me. I look at Lavender's flat dead face and pray she'd open her eyes and look up at me. But she doesn't. She is absolutely dead. There is no hope.

So I do the next best thing. I stand, clench my fist, hold it up to Mack's filthy face, and yell, "It's all your fault, you dirty bum!"

"Huh?" he says, stepping back.

Tears are streaming down into my mouth. "I'm gonna beat the shit outta you!" I scream.

"Matt, no!" yells Mimi, grabbing my arm.

Mack turns and runs. But his left foot catches a lump of dog shit and down he skids. On his knees, gasping for air, he finally lifts himself and scrambles toward the door, but his right foot steps on another pile of shit, and he falls hard. He picks himself up with shit smeared all over his pants and hands. Slowly, he limps out the door, into the hallway.

Everything is so pathetic.

I kneel beside Lavender and gently roll her back onto her belly, like we found her. Life sucks.

"I'm sorry, girl," I say, burying my head into her dirty yellow fur. This is going to break Sailor Barlow's poor heart. In my stupid optimism, everything had gone so perfectly: I'd look for a dog, find a dog, take a picture of a dog, show dog to Barlow — happy ending.

But it didn't go that way.

I failed my friend, the Champ. And there's not a damn thing I can do about it.

When I compose myself, I stroke Lavender's matted fur and think about taking my finger and pushing her wiener-sausage eye back into its socket where it belongs. But I decide not to.

I reach into my pants pocket, pull out a dog biscuit, and place it beside her head. I then take my camera and snap her picture.

"She looks at peace," says Mimi. Her eyes are moist.

"Like she's sleeping."

There's nothing else to do, so I bend down, scoop her up, and hold her in my arms.

"Now what?" asks Mimi.

As usual, I don't have a clue. We walk outta Barlow's apartment, me cradling Lavender in my arms, close to my chest.

"Shouldn't we bury her?" says Mimi, closing the door and pocketing the key.

"Where?"

"Central Park?"

I shake my head. Too far uptown.

"Don't we need to wrap her in something?" she says, stepping out onto the sidewalk.

I spot Mack's seat cushion, the ripped canvas.

"How 'bout that?" I say, pointing with my chin.

Mimi bends down, picks it up, and unfolds it. Suddenly, she freezes. "Matt!" she gasps. "Look!"

She flips open the canvas, which is about five feet by three feet. It's a beautiful painting of a young boy sitting on a porch reading a letter. On his lap are three unopened letters. On the bottom is the painter's signature: BENNY BARLOW.

Written on back of the painting, in bold block letters, is the title: *The Two Hardest Things to Handle in Life – Failure and Success.*

How does a young boy reading a letter on a porch relate to failure and success?

Chapter 36

I GO UPSTAIRS TO MY bedroom and hide Barlow's rolled up painting under my bed. Gram's out shopping at A&P and forgot her shopping list, which is laying on my desk: ground beef, Hamburger Helper, milk, Pepsi, peas, carrots, onions, Ring Dings. Next to her list is a letter written on hotel stationary. Stamp-marked Lisbon, Portugal.

> *Dear Matthew,*
>
> *I am SO disappointed in you! I know we've been gone longer than expected, but that can't be helped, and this doesn't mean you should be misbehaving! Do Jack and I need to fly back home to discipline you? Why aren't you doing your daily chores as we agreed? Why are you spending so much time away from home? Why are you acting like a spoiled little brat? Are you, at least, attending summer school? I am horrified! Gram feels you are "walking down the wrong road." After all I have been through, I cannot weather another tragedy. CLEAN UP YOUR ACT AND YOUR ROOM!*
>
> *Shocked and dismayed,*
> *Mother*

"Mom, the road I'm walking on is called the Bowery," I whisper. "It's a dirty, nasty road, but it's the road I've chosen."

Chapter 37

IVAN KARP, THE OWNER OF OK Harris Gallery, lays the canvas flat on his desk. His bushy eyebrows lift as he bends down to inspect it. The young boy painted on the canvas is still sitting on the porch reading his letter, and his legs are still too short to reach the wooden floor. A pot of blue morning glories hangs behind his shoulder, and a golden wheat field sways in the breeze.

"Arhumm…," he says, hunched over the painting.

Mimi and I look at each other.

"Mmurhh…," he says, pressing his fingers into his cheeks.

Art is cluttered all over his gallery walls, the floor, the ceiling—art of every size, crazy shape, and description.

"Mmmurum…" Karp's wearing a Detroit Tigers baseball cap and a thin cigar's sticking out of his mouth.

"This painting is…absolutely wonderful!"

Mimi and I smile.

"Actually," he says, "I'm stunned." He touches the painting, almost caresses it. "What makes it special is the juicy brushwork and the sunlight splashing onto the boy's face…Where'd you get it?"

"Found it," I say.

"Actually, I found it," corrects Mimi.

"Where?"

"On the sidewalk."

Karp's eyes slide up. "Sidewalk?"

"Under a panhandler's butt," clarifies Mimi. "It was his seat cushion."
I elbow her to shut up.

"A panhandler's seat cushion?" says Karp, squinting.

"Yup!" She nods. "Just lying on the sidewalk, folded under his ass."
I elbow her. Karp doesn't need to know details.

"Hackensack Mack is his name," she says.

Mr. Karp looks at her, puzzled.

"It's hidden treasure, right here on the Bowery, under his stinky butt!"

Mr. Karp keeps looking at her, and then pulls the cigar from his mouth. "You just—"

"Picked it up off the sidewalk," smiles Mimi. "Great story, isn't it?"

"The Bowery is an unlikely place to find a painting."

"But it's true," she says.

"It's not credible," he laughs. He sits down, leans back in his chair, and stares at the wall beyond Mimi's head.

"You don't believe me, do you?" she says.

I elbow her again.

Karp looks up at the ceiling and rotates his cigar with his fingers. He sits that way for a long time thinking. Then he looks back at the painting, inspecting its frayed border, a small rip on the side, and a few scratches in the corner. I don't know how to read him, but I feel we're striking out.

"Actually," I say, pitch-hitting, "the artist is my friend."

"Really now?" he grins. It's a shit-eating grin.

I nod.

"So why isn't your friend here, with us now?"

"You don't believe us, do you?" says Mimi.

He taps his fingers on the top of his desk. "So where is this *friend*?"

"In the hospital," says Mimi, "if you really must know." She's sounding a bit too nasty, and Karp puckers his mouth and throws her a look. I don't think he likes her attitude.

"Mr. Karp," she says, "you obviously don't understand the significance of this wonderful painting we brought you this afternoon."

"No," he grins, "but I get the feeling you're going to tell me."

"This painting," she says, pointing, "was painted by a world champion boxer!"

He grins. "I know that, missy. You don't think I know that? I was ringside the night Joe Louis put the old horse puncher on his ass."

139

Mimi leans back in her chair. "Oh."

We sit quiet.

Karp starts rotating his unlit cigar with his hand again. "Benny "Sailor" Barlow started painting in Europe after retiring from the ring. Did you know that?" He then starts leafing through papers cluttered on his desk. I feel we're losing him.

"Mr. Barlow," I say, leaning forward, "is my good friend. I met him the day he was found lying on the street."

Karp looks at me. "Yeah, I read about that."

"He's ill," I continue. "Paint fumes—boxing—drugs, alcohol. We came to you because we thought..."

"...I could help you."

"Well...help *him*."

Mr. Karp nods. "His brain's probably rattled—happens to painters who don't ventilate and fighters who get punched."

"Please help him."

"You want me to show this painting?" he asks, placing his elbows on his cluttered desk.

"Or give him a show or advertise it." But I know that's all kind of pointless for one painting.

He looks down at Barlow's painting. "It's in pretty rough shape. It can be cleaned and repaired, I guess. Are there other paintings?"

I shrug. "Sort of."

"Sort of?" he says. "That's a yes-or-no question."

"The answer to your yes-or-no question is *sort of* yes and no," smiles Mimi.

Karp's eyes cut to Mimi and he frowns. "Oh, we're playing word games, are we, sweetie?"

She smiles flirtatiously.

He looks down at the Champ's painting again and shakes his head. "I love this painting. But my gut tells me there's something fishy here."

"On the other hand, maybe your gut isn't too bright," quips Mimi.

He looks at her for a long time, tapping his fingers on his desk. He then grins. "True. It mostly knows when it wants a good corn beef sandwich from Katz's Deli."

Mimi and I chuckle politely at his joke.

But our meeting is officially over. Mr. Karp rolls up Barlow's painting, sticks it in a circular casing, and hands it back to me. "Not much I can do with one painting, my friend. But I do have an opening in November. If you find nine more Barlow originals hiding under Hackensack Mack's slinky butt, contact me."

He then looks over at Mimi and tips his baseball cap. "You're a spunky little minx, ain't ya?"

"A regular spitfire," says Mimi, grinning.

Once we hit the street, I turn to Mimi. "You jerk! You blew it!"

Mimi smiles from ear to ear. "You kidding me? We nailed it! Karp is hooked!"

"Are you kidding me? He almost threw you out!"

"Listen to me. That man is sucked in by the backstory I painted for him! Lost treasure hiding under Hackensack Mack's butt! What a dramatic story! Television, radio, magazines will eat it up!"

Maybe she's right.

We just need to find nine more Barlow originals.

Chapter 38

THE CHAMP IS HOLDING LAVENDER'S photo close to his flat-nosed face, gently petting it. "She sick?"

I put a finger to my lips and smile. "Sshh! She's sleeping."

He tilts the photo left and right. It's a good photo of her furry backside. She doesn't look dead—just flat.

"Why she sleepin' in the bathroom?" he mumbles.

"Your apartment's being cleaned," I lie. I can be a pretty good liar when I wanna be. "So she's in there just till it's finished."

"Skinny," he says. His voice is garbled, like most punch-drunk fighters.

I hope Lavender's photo will keep him company. It must be awful lonely lying in a hospital bed all day. He props the photo against his plastic water pitcher so he can see her when he wakes up in the morning.

I point to the dog biscuit I strategically placed beside her head.

"Hi, girl," he says at the photo. "Mack feedin' ya? He's simple-minded sometime. You and him my best friends. When I get outta here…"

That's when Wanda and Doctor Roth walk in. Barlow holds up Lavender's photo and smiles proudly. Doctor Roth smiles back to be polite, then checks Barlow's pulse. Wanda sticks a thermometer in Barlow's mouth.

"Champ," the doctor says with a smile, resting his hand on Barlow's shoulder, "you're as strong as an ox."

Barlow lifts his arm and makes a fist. "Moo!"

"Not every ex-boxer who comes into St. Vincent's makes such a dramatic turnaround."

Barlow smiles.

"I think Mr. Barlow has a lot more living to do," says Wanda, shaking the thermometer. "Perhaps the Champ has some unfinished business to attend to?"

Barlow looks at me.

Wanda says, "He do his roadwork every morning now. Last week he made it to the end of the floor and back. Didn't you, Champ?"

He smiles. "Five times."

Doctor Roth looks at me. His eyes are dark and steady. He's a tall fiftyish Dr. Kildare with heavy eyebrows and a full head of brown hair combed straight back. His square jaw is cleanly shaven. "Are you the young man who informed us about paint poisoning?" he asks.

"Yes, sir."

"We would've eventually diagnosed it," he says, "but thank you anyway. Your concern is most admirable. May I speak with you outside in the hallway?"

Dr. Roth, Wanda, and I walk into the corridor. I take Barlow's rolled-up painting with me.

"Matthew," Dr. Roth says softly, "Mr. Barlow has withstood a considerable amount of cerebral trauma. He's been punched numerous times about his head, and I don't need to tell you that's not healthy. His CAT scan shows severe cerebral atrophy, enlarged ventricles filled with fluid, and a deep tunnel-like cave in the septum."

"What's that mean?" I ask.

"It means his brain is rapidly shrinking. Dead brain cells are dissolving like sugar in water. Neurological tests show severely impaired short-term memory and motor skills."

"Will he get better?"

Dr. Roth and Wanda glance at each other, then he asks me to follow them. We enter an elevator, and Wanda pushes the down button. When the door opens, we turn left and enter a dark room where a man in bed is gently wobbling. His nose is flat, like Barlow's, and he's staring at an empty wall. It doesn't look like he's aware we're standing here.

"Meet Mr. Pacheco," whispers Roth, "another ex-boxer."

"He once boxed Sugar Ray Robinson," whispers Wanda.

"Soon, Mr. Barlow will be joining him. They both will continue to receive special care at another facility, but I'm afraid the damage has already been done. It's irreversible. Mr. Barlow will be an invalid from here on out."

"Will he ever be able to go back home?"

"Doubtful," says Dr. Roth. "Mr. Barlow's been with us this long because a special team of neurologists have been studying sports-related brain abnormalities. The neuro-psychologist examining him says he's approaching second-stage dementia, very similar to Alzheimer's. His connection to reality will become increasingly fragile."

"He's on a downward spiral," says Wanda, nodding. "Soon he be needin' help shaving, showering, and putting on slippers. Soon, diapers."

I grimace.

"Already I'm cutting his meat into little pieces so he won't choke," she says. "This mornin', I had to coax him to eat somethin' besides chocolate pudding. He loves his chocolate pudding."

"So," I say, pointing to Mr. Pacheco, "this is gonna h-happen to the Champ?"

Dr. Roth rubs the back of his neck. "Mr. Barlow is very lucky to be alive. I meant what I had said earlier — he's as strong as an ox — but his brain injuries are extensive. He'll have good days and bad. His lucidity will fluctuate. From here on out, he'll need around-the-clock medical attention."

Mr. Pacheco, as far as I can tell, isn't in pain, but he's definitely in his own shadowy dream world. The same is going to happen to Barlow?

"What do you have there?" asks Wanda, changing the subject.

I unroll Barlow's canvas. The young boy is still looking down, reading the letter he holds in his hands.

"Did Mr. Barlow paint this?" asks Wanda.

I nod.

Her eyes widen. "You sure?"

Dr. Roth looks astonished.

"I cleaned it up and had it appraised," I say.

"Where?" asks Dr. Roth.

"OK Harris."

They both look at each other.

"That's a prestigious gallery," he says. "Did they price it for you?"

I nod.

"And?" he asks.

I tell him.

He reaches for the painting. "May I take a look? I appreciate good art." We step outside and he gently places the canvas on a counter. He leans over and begins studying it. He says Barlow's painting has voluptuous vitality and visceral force, whatever that means. And he likes the shadows and the somber mood conveyed within the composition.

"It looks like a Hoper," say Wanda.

"I think you mean Hopper," corrects Roth, "an Edward Hopper, only better."

Chapter 39

I UNFURL THE PAINTING AND hold it close to Barlow's face. "Who's the b-boy?"

He leans forward and touches it, just like he did with Lavender's photo. Then he looks at me and smiles. "You know damn well who that is."

"I do?"

"That's you!"

At first I think he's pulling my leg, but I quickly see he's dead serious. He starts talking to me like I'm his son! He doesn't even have a son—the papers said nothing about a son.

It's all very awkward and weird.

"Luke," he says, "Don'cha'member them boots? Bought 'em for ya! Was the first thing come outta my purse afta the Louis fight."

I just look at him, embarrassed. He's seeing someone who isn't here.

"Wish ya been there fer that fight. Woulda been proud o' your old man, even though I lost. Bought 'em next mornin'."

This conversation is so damn pathetic. I feel heartbroken for him. "Thanks, Dad," I say.

Suddenly his life starts spilling out of him. He's talking to either me or Luke, but I don't care. I just lean forward and listen to the bits and drabs that eventually come out of his mouth.

I sit hypnotized.

I learn Barlow grew up the son of dirt-poor Arkansas alfalfa farmers. He made his first punching bag out of a cow's bladder. That busted, so he rigged up a pillowcase stuffed with rags. That worked better, until it split. Then he found an old mattress, wrapped it around a tree with rope, and punched it until it wore out.

There are long pauses when he forgets a word, but they eventually trickle out, soft and mushed. I'm in no hurry.

He was ten when he won his first amateur bout. At eleven, he was winning three-round battles at county fairs, church carnivals, and in local saloons. At thirteen, he won his first Golden Gloves title and local boxing people started noticing this handsome kid who threw a heavy punch and had an appetite for fighting. With the blessing of his parents, he left school and turned pro. He mailed home money when he could.

By eighteen, Barlow was traveling the country, climbing the light heavyweight ladder. With amazing clarity, he describes training camps, four-round preliminary bouts, eight-round co-main events, and ten-round main events at the Boston Garden, and in Madison Square Garden.

I lean on the edge of my chair spellbound, hanging on to every garbled word that crawls out of his mouth.

So do the two pigeons sitting on his window sill.

I learn how promoters short-change fighters' purses, and how Barlow washed his face with his own piss to toughen his skin.

One night in San Francisco, Barlow's trainer, a guy named Panama, removed the horse-hair padding from Barlow's gloves, making them rock hard. That night, Barlow broke his opponent's nose, fractured both of his cheekbones, and punched him into a coma. He died three days later.

Barlow grins and points to the jagged scars over both of his eyes and on the bridge of his nose. I learn what I already knew: boxing is ugly.

"Ugly, all right." He looks at his gnarled hands in his lap. "Ain't no life for a young'un. Besides, your mother…well…I know I ain't always been there for ya…" A pained expression twists onto his battered face.

"It's okay, Dad," I say, softly patting his shoulder.

"No, Luke…ain't…I'd write ya letters and send ya money, but…" His voice trails off.

I feel a sudden lump of emotion in my throat, and start thinking about my own father. *Where are you, Dad? Do you love me?*

I look at the Champ; there's scar tissue on his face, but a lot more in his heart. "I love you, Dad," I say.

His hand reaches out for mine. "I robbed ya, Luke. I shoulda been there for ya…selfish…" The Champ begins weeping. I look at him sobbing, and I see my mother and father crying for Daniel.

147

"It's okay, Dad," I say, fighting back tears. I'm not so good with emotions, and this is a lot more emotion than I'm used to—it's a perfect time to change channels. "Dad, tell me about the night you won the light heavyweight title. I wish I was there."

He tilts his head. "But you was there."

"I just wanna hear it again."

It's like the sun suddenly burst out—a smile appears on his face. Drying his eyes, he recalls the magical night he shook the world. "Well," he slurs, "Maxie had me down in the first. Again in the…third, and in the…fifth. Everyone thought I was a goner, including me. I just hadda hang on, is all. Then in the…thirteenth, I'm all busted up, bleedin', and we come outta a clench and I step to his left and see my opening—Wham!"

"Down he goes!" I guess.

"Like a sack a potatas!"

Exhausted, the Champ slumps back in bed.

"Hooray! My dad became the light heavyweight champion of the world!"

"After the fight, we hug and kiss."

I could never understand why boxers do that. So I ask him.

He looks out the window at the two pigeons listening in.

"Well…don't exactly know…Maybe it's 'cause our souls kinda touch in there. Huggin' a guy afterwards is like huggin' yourself, cuz ya seein' all the strong things in him that's probably in you."

He sits back up and grabs his chocolate pudding. He swallows a few spoonfuls and then sets it down. "Yeah, boxin's ugly, but sometimes it's beootiful."

He looks back at the little boy reading the letter in his painting. "Son, I wrote ya alotta letters. I don't blame ya for never writin' back. She kept you away." He yawns, closes his eyes, and falls asleep.

I look at the Champ's painting. *The Hardest Thing to Handle in Life is Success and Failure.* It's beginning to make sense.

Chapter 40

A VASE OF BLUE MORNING glories sits on the window sill when I visit the Champ three days later. But Barlow looks horrible — he's slumped in a chair, hair mussed, eyes cloudy. Is he drifting into Mr. Pacheco's shadowy dream world?

"How's The Brown Bomber?" he slurs. His crooked smile and cloudy eyes make me sick to my stomach. "I fought him, ya know."

"Wanna play checkers?" I say, sitting down on his bed. "Brought some checkers, thought we'd play some checkers."

He just sits here, stagnant. I bite my lower lip and fight back tears. When you get involved in someone else's life, get ready for pain.

Wanda walks in and smiles. "Hi, Matthew!" She's holding a plastic cup of chocolate pudding. "Checking in on our Champ?"

I nod.

"Unfortunately, today isn't one of his better days." She snaps a paper bib around his neck and hands him his pudding. She softly massages his shoulders while she helps him spoon it into his mouth. "After Mr. Barlow finish his snack," she says, "let's you and me have a little chitchat outside."

I nod.

Wanda's sweet flutelike voice isn't so flutelike this afternoon. I figure, our little chitchat isn't gonna be good.

Outside, two chairs are already pulled up. We sit down, side by side, and she reaches out to hold my hands. She tells me from now on I shouldn't expect much from the Champ. It's very sweet of me to bring flowers and pizza and checkers, but for most of his remaining days, he will be incapable of clear thinking. She says he's gotten into the dangerous habit of wandering off at night in remote areas of the hospital. Last night, a security guard pulled him out of a storage closet.

"When they found him, he was on his hands and knees, crying. He be searching for his lost dog," says Wanda, softly. "Doctor Roth feels from now on we need to tether him to his bed."

"Tether?"

"Tie him down."

"Oh, shit. When will he be moving in with Mr. Pacheco?"

"Oh, dear," she says. "Mr. Pacheco died yesterday."

I take all of this in with pretended calm, saying things like "uh-huh" and "okay," but sadness is exploding inside me. I've been in deep denial, quitting baseball and committing myself to nursing the Champ back to health with flowers and pizza and checkers, and maybe a prayer or two, but that's just plain stupid. You can't pray away death.

"On a more positive note"-- she smiles--"he had a visitor yesterday. A Mr. Karp. He left a big vase of blue flowers."

"Yeah, I saw."

"Matthew, you've been a good friend. But I think it's time for you to go." She reaches over to hug me, and wipe the tears from my eyes. "Say good-bye to your friend."

When I walk into the Champ's room, he's shadowboxing, shirtless. His wide shoulders, long arms, and a battleship tattooed on his chest are lacquered with sweat as he bobs and weaves from side to side. Left hooks and right crosses are curving through the air. Who is he fighting— The Brown Bomber? Maxie Johansson?

"Not bad, huh?" he mutters.

"You look real good, Champ," I say.

"Panama, ya shouldn't a cut them gloves. I coulda took him without ya doing that."

I realize I'm talking to a young Sailor Barlow after a fight he fought decades ago.

"Champ," says Panama, "I didn't wanna take a chance you getting hurt."

"I killed him, Panama. Shouldn't a punched them horses either."

Panama nods.

150

"I'm a painter now," he says.

"I heard."

"Paintin'…fun…happy…"

"I heard you paint good," says Panama.

"They stole my paintings."

I nearly jump! "Who stole your paintings?"

"Promoters stole from us, Panama—"

I try to snap him back into the present. "Did Funny Fred steal your paintings?"

The Champ's sweaty face is blank and his damaged brain is wobbling back and forth through decades.

"Champ, who stole your paintings? Fred? Norman?"

He sits down. "People lie 'n steal."

I kneel down in front of him. The money from his paintings is his money—not Funny Fred's or Norman's, or anybody else's. That money should be bringing him security and peace at the end of his life so he won't die in some flophouse.

I rest my hands on his knees. "Dad, look at me, Dad."

His eyes widen, and he leans back, blinking. It's like I've magically appeared, like a ghost, before him.

"Dad, who stole your paintings?"

"They didn't steal 'em all, Luke."

"What do you mean?"

"There's a spot—"

"A spot?"

"My secret hidin' spot…" He blinks a few times, then looks at the blue morning glories sitting on the window sill.

"Where, Dad? Where?"

He looks back at Luke and grins. "In my apartment—I'll show ya."

There's nothing in that damn apartment but a dirty mattress, a long kitchen table, and dog shit…

Holy shit! The mattress!

Chapter 41

ODAY MY ONE-IN-A-MILLION SECRET PLAN goes into action. But it's dead in the water as soon as I enter the Champ's room. A strange woman is lying in his bed.

"W-Where's Mr. Barlow?"

"Who?"

I walk to the nurse's desk. "Where's Mr. Barlow?"

"Not now. I'm busy," says a freckle-faced nurse, trotting away.

Another nurse, sitting behind the counter keeps me waiting for like an hour. Finally she says, without bothering to look up at me, "Okay, who is it you want?"

"Mr. Benny Barlow—the man who was in room four-one-one."

She flips a few papers, then looks up at me. "Sorry. I'm new to this floor."

"Where's Wanda?"

"Day off." Then she walks away.

I begin to panic. Is he dead? Ten minutes pass before I find an attendant willing to tell me where the Champ is—Room 214.

I press the down button, and hear the old gypsy woman whisper: *"Boyo, a dark shadow's falling over you. Your friend's in Mr. Pacheco's room—dead."*

My heart's hammering in my chest, my head's pounding. I step out of the elevator and see another attendant wheeling a body on a gurney. I know he's dead because a tag is dangling from his toe. I lift the sheet.

"Whoa!" says the attendant. "Don't touch!"

"That's Benny Barlow, isn't it?"

He nods. "Died of a broken heart, boyo."

Why do I always create these horrible nightmares in my head?

When I walk into Room 214, Barlow is snoring. His right wrist is chained to the metal railing.

I drop my duffle bag to the floor, and a young nurse squeaks in. "Who are you?" she says.

"His son, Luke."

She checks her clipboard and looks up. "You're name's not here."

"It's okay. Wanda and Dr. Roth know me. He was just transferred from the fourth floor." It takes two people to make a lie work: the person who tells it, and the person who believes it. "Okay." She shrugs.

"Would it be possible," I say with a smile, "if when my dad wakes up, I take him for a little stroll?"

"Fine with me," she says. Before leaving, she releases his wrist from the restraint. "Just keep him on this floor."

As soon as she leaves, I yank him up, swing his legs out of bed, and walk him to the bathroom.

"Huh?" he says, confused.

"We're doing roadwork," I say, closing the door behind me.

"Wass happenin'?" he says, slumped on the toilet seat.

My heart races as I open my duffle bag and pull out my father's clothing: a starched white shirt, gray dress pants, black shoes, and socks. I found all his stuff dumped in our basement, in a cardboard box labeled Discard.

"Put these on!" This is the most stupidest or bestest thing I've ever done—I don't know which—but I do know kidnapping is a criminal offense and will land my ass in jail.

"You're doing roadwork," I say, kneeling down to slip my father's black nylon sock onto the Champ's foot. My secret plan depends on finding nine more paintings.

"I ain't goin'," he growls, glaring at me. It's probably the same glare he gave Joe Louis in the ring.

"Champ," I whisper, "I'm not taking you anywhere—you're taking me to your secret hiding spot, where you hid your paintings."

Please, let there be nine more paintings!

"Who're you?" he slurs.

"C'mon, you remember me — flowers, pizza, checkers?"

He scowls, clenches his fist, and cocks back his arm. I'm getting punched any second now.

"Dad! It's me, Luke!"

His face twists in confusion, and he lowers his arm.

I quickly lift his leg and slip my father's sock onto his other foot.

"You ain't Luke," he mutters, pulling his leg away.

"Dad, you wrote me letters all the time, remember? You even painted me reading those letters."

He scratches his head and looks puzzled. "Yeah, well…no, Luke, I ain't goin' nowhere."

But I insist. I hold my father's white dress shirt up so he can stick his arms through the sleeves.

"Lemme alone," he mumbles. "I'm tired, Luke."

I gotta get the Champ out of this damn hospital. He's one step from croaking like Mr. Pacheco, and I gotta rescue him. It might sound crazy, and maybe I'm just getting my false hopes up, but the only way I can help the Champ is by rescuing his paintings. Some thief is robbing him blind, and I'm not gonna let it continue. Rescuing his paintings is rescuing the Champ. Those paintings are all he has left in this world. His health and dignity are gone, but his paintings will sell for millions and put him back into the spotlight where he belongs. But most importantly, his paintings will restore his dignity.

If there are paintings.

"Ain't goin'." He crosses his arms and kicks off the socks.

"C'mon, Dad! You're making your comeback today! The world is waiting!"

"No!"

I know lying to the Champ and kidnapping is dead wrong, and I feel guilty and all, but screw it. I have to do it. For him.

"Dad, please, let's go. Lavender misses you."

My last sentence is pure magic! It's genius!

Barlow strips off his pajamas and steps into my father's pants. He even laces up his shoes by himself! The clothes don't fit perfectly, but it works. I tuck in his shirt, comb his hair, and he's good to go.

I open the bathroom door, we step down the hallway, and then into the stairwell.

"Where we goin'?" he repeats.

I hold his arm as we descend the gray-painted stairwell. "I already told you, Dad. Don't you remember?"

Silence.

I push him through the hospital lobby, and through the revolving front door. We walk down 14th Street to the corner. As we walk down the subway steps, I continue holding his arm. I don't want him to fall or get lost. It's best we stay connected.

"I remember now—Lavender!" he says.

I just hope he remembers his secret hiding spot.

If there is a secret hiding spot.

We walk into a waiting subway car and sit down. The Champ is breathing hard.

Part of me is saying, *Matt, stop! This is insane!* But I never was too good at listening to myself.

I can see the headline now: YOUNG BOY — SEEKING PAINTINGS — KIDNAPS BENNY "SAILOR" BARLOW.

Chapter 42

BARLOW'S STRIDE IS GRACEFULLY CLUMSY, and after a few blocks, he starts talking in full sentences instead of grunts and monosyllables. Excitement is written all over his old dented face, and he's even pulling back his shoulders while walking. The Champ is thrilled to be seeing his dog again.

Except there is no dog.

His voice stumbles over words. "She likes me scratchin' behind her ears." He chuckles. "The sides o' her mouth curl up, and her tongue hangs out, like she's smilin'."

But I'm not smiling. I'm bleeding my brain to the bone, trying to come up with a good excuse to tell him about his dead dog.

After walking two blocks, I learn more stuff about the Champ. At the end of his boxing career he adopted Lavender in London. "She kept me company." By then, he was a paunchy heavyweight, a human punching bag, who traveled through Europe getting beat up twice a month by young heavyweights. Lavender, his new furry traveling companion, licked his wounds.

"The night I got knocked out in Paris, they carried me out on a stretcher, and I woke up in the hospital with a busted jaw." The next day, Barlow reinvented himself. "I walked into an art shop and bought me some brushpaints."

"You had no formal art training?" I ask.

"Nah. I ain't contaminated with no education."

"Amazing."

"My mother was an artist."

"Really?"

"Quilts."

"She teach you?"

"Nah. Art just flow outta my brushpaint and onto the canvas without me gettin' in the way."

"Wow!"

"Yeah, paintin' just come natural." He laughs. "Just changed one canvas for another."

As we walk closer to the Bowery, holding each other's hand, I can see the Champ become more alert and wheezy-breathing with excitement. It's like he's emerging from hibernation. With each step, I watch a droopy old man turn into an eager little kid going home to see his dog.

His dead dog—which Mimi and I threw in a dumpster.

A man walks up to us, smiling. "Hey, Sailor! How ya doin'?"

"Not bad."

"Can I have your autograph?" He hands the Champ a pen and paper. Barlow signs his name and hands it back. This time his signature is a little bit better than a squiggly line.

The Champ turns to me and grins. "People 'member me better'n I 'member myself."

Dr. Roth and Wanda were wrong about Sailor Barlow. They mean well, but the Champ isn't on death's door. Doctors and nurses can be wrong, you know. Recently, I read about a doctor diagnosing a baby with a cancerous brain tumor. But guess what? It wasn't malignant or cancerous at all. It was a human foot growing inside the kid's head! How disgusting is that? Well, the point is, sometimes doctors don't know squat. That's a fact.

Ever since we snuck out of the hospital, the Champ and I were holding hands. It feels good being connected to boxing greatness.

I wish Mimi was here. She'd get a big kick out of this!

As we approach Barlow's apartment, I begin wondering: Why did Barlow feel so much passion for a dog but not his own son? Is loving a dog easier? Does my dad love music more than me? Is music easier to love than a son? It hurts to think I'm playing second fiddle to my dad's music, no pun intended. Deep down, I think I'm a pretty good kid. I'm somewhat lovable, I'm strong sometimes, I'm brave every once in a while, and I'm semi-smart.

Why did my father leave me? I know he's alcoholic, but did something scar him when he was young? Did he play second fiddle to his father? Did my grandfather play second fiddle to his father? Am I the product of a long line of second fiddlers? *Aw, screw me – I think too much.*

When we finally reach the Champ's brownstone, he looks up and down the street. "Where is she?" he asks.

"Maybe with Hackensack Mack."

He's shaking his head as he opens the black door and walks up the narrow staircase, which still smells of piss and paint. He tells me to stop holding his hand. "I ain't no baby," he says pulling away.

"Lavender! Lavender!" he calls.

I stick the key in the lock and open the door. The apartment is the same – empty. Only the dirty mattress, the long wooden table, and dog crap. I kneel down and check the mattress…nothing.

The Champ looks out the window, wheezing. "Where's my dog?"

I look under the mattress…nothing. I rip it open…nothing.

"Champ, where's your secret hiding spot?"

"Where's my dog?"

I knock on the plaster walls, I stomp on the wooden floors. Nothing.

"Champ," I say, "there is no secret hiding spot, is there?"

"Mack hates my dog."

"Well…maybe that nice lady across the hall is walking Lavender with her dog."

"Naah," he wheezes.

Me and my stupid one-in-a-million secret plan.

Then he turns and walks over to the wooden table in the middle of the room. "I'm worried," he says, rubbing his square jaw. He might start crying any second.

"We'll find her," I lie.

Then he places his hands on the table and begins shaking it violently. Anger and sadness are exploding out of him. He won't stop shaking the damn table. It's like he wants to kill it.

"What're you doing?" I say.

His face is red and scrunched up, like he's having a convulsion. He keeps shaking, pulling, and yelling at the table!

"Pull!" he orders, pointing with his chin to the other side of the table. "*Pull!*"

I run to the other side and pull, like him, with both hands. We begin yanking the table in opposite directions — I think that's what he wants. After eight sharp tugs, the table cracks open with a rusty screeeeech! and I'm knocked to the floor. After I stand up and wipe the dry dog shit from the back of my pants, I smell fresh paint fumes. I look down into the table and see a sunken compartment crammed with canvases — some rolled up, but most lying flat.

I pick up the top canvas. Written on the back, in block letters, is the painting's title: *A Songwriter at Work.* I flip it around and stare at a man wearing a white shirt and blue tie sitting at a piano. He's hunched over the keyboard, eyes closed, playing a melody.

I gulp and my throat goes dry.

Holy shit! It's a painting of my father.

Chapter 43

THE CHAMP AND I STUMBLE across the street to the Blarney Stone, push through the front door and sit in a booth. Our ingenious hospital escape, quick subway ride, unsuccessful dog search, and fantastic artistic discovery has exhausted poor old Barlow.

"So," I say, carefully laying the canvases flat on the table, "you know George Watt?"

"Yeah."

"How?"

But he's already asleep, burbling little snores, swallowed up in my dad's old baggy clothing.

Ms. Hanover walks over and sits across from me. "Let him rest," she whispers. Then she looks down at the top painting — of my father. She gently touches it and starts whistling my dad's song "You're Mine Always."

We look at each other.

"You know my father's song?"

She looks at the painting. "Yes…I've met your father."

"When?"

"Well…he sometimes stops in."

My jaw drops. "Here? Why didn't you tell me?"

She touches the painting, and then looks up at me. "Well, it took me awhile to piece it all together."

"He comes in here?"

"Once or twice."

"You should've told me."

Funny Fred walks from the back. "Slide over, Ping," he says. "Well, look what the cat's dragged in—Benny and the 'connected-to-royalty' boy!"

I sneer. "You again?"

He grins. "Where better to study the downtrodden?"

The Champ continues snoring.

Funny Fred looks at the Champ's paintings, then at Ms. Hanover. "Looks like a few got away."

Ms. Hanover looks at Funny Fred. A brief uncertainty flashes in her eyes. Then it's gone.

Funny Fred is wearing a brand new sports jacket with big brown buttons, and a stupid red polka-dot-thingy is sticking out from his breast pocket. He has *thief* written all over his face.

"How many canvases here?" he asks casually.

I don't say anything—I just look at his thin pasty face.

He starts counting.

"Nice jacket, Fred," I say. "How much it cost?"

He's too busy counting to answer.

Just watching his itchy paws touch the Champ's paintings pisses me off. How many paintings did this weasel steal—probably with his disgusting friend, Norman…and Ms. Hanover? My mind begins racing. Is she involved? I look down at her Born to Raise Hell tattoo.

Funny Fred counts. Ms. Hanover is looking at me.

I say, "Somebody'll make a boatload of money, those paintings."

Without looking up, he says, "Noticed my new Scottish tweed, huh?"

"Expensive?"

He ignores my question and glances over at the Champ. "Benny, you dumb bastard—how could you have…?"

"Hey, asshole," I interrupt, "you ever been convicted of a crime?"

"Excuse you?" he says, looking up.

"Ever been in jail? Like for stealing?"

His eyes cut to Ms. Hanover. She bites her lower lip, realizes she's doing it, and stops.

"You stole Barlow's paintings, didn't you?" It's not really a question.

He glances at Ms. Hanover again, and then leans toward me. "Pardon me?"

"You're a f-fucking thief!"

"Matthew! Stop!" she hisses.

"He stole Barlow's paintings!"

Ms. Hanover's eyes scan the room.

The Champ starts grumbling. "No, Panama...shouldn't a done it." I elbow him to shut up.

Funny Fred leans toward me. "You serious?"

I slap his claws off the Champ's paintings. "You're a thieving prick!" People stare at us.

"You have some big set of gonads, little boy," he says.

"Admit it!" I spit. It feels good yelling into his face. He's busted! He suddenly begins laughing.

"What's so damn funny, asshole?" I shout.

"Matthew! Quiet!" says Ms. Hanover, reaching across the table to grab my arm.

I pull away. "And you helped him—didn't you?"

"You're mistaken," she says.

"No I'm not. You helped him!"

She shakes her head.

"Admit it!"

"We already know who stole his paintings," she says.

I look at her.

"His neighbor."

The head banger?

"A woman," she says.

"She own a dog?" I ask.

Funny Fred nods. He takes in a long deep breath and composes himself. "Mrs. Huerta, a woman with a German shepherd across the hall. She recently sublet her apartment and moved back to Spain. When Barlow's paintings started popping up in Barcelona and Madrid, I figured out her scam. I'm an aesthete, remember, who keeps tabs on the art world."

"*El Prado* has already purchased one of Barlow's cityscapes," adds Ms. Hanover. "We've already contacted the museum and police."

I feel my cheeks grow hot with embarrassment. I'm too ashamed to even look at them, but when I do, I'm even more ashamed. "I'm a stupid idiot. Sorry."

"No harm done," says Funny Fred. "You put a scare into me. But I admire the way you stood up for Benny like that. You're a valiant friend." He looks over at Ms. Hanover. "I truly thought the little son of a bitch was gonna clobber me!"

I don't feel like a valiant friend — whatever *valiant* means. I feel like a jackass.

"Actually, I wish you had clobbered me, then I'd be connected to boxing royalty!"

Ms. Hanover straightens the napkin holder on the table and changes the subject. "Fred, you know who Matthew's father is, don't you?"

Funny Fred looks at my face, and then down at Barlow's painting. He looks back up at me again and snaps his fingers. "I knew it!"

"A very talented writer, your father," says Ms. Hanover, softly, "I'm sure he's an inspiration to you."

"Was..."

They quickly glance at each other.

"...until he vanished."

"I know where he is," she says. She looks at me for a long time, then points to a photograph hanging on the wall directly above our heads.

I look up.

It's a photo of Frank Sinatra and Ella Fitzgerald leaning against a piano. The pianist in the background is my father. And he's smiling down at me.

Chapter 44

WHY D-DIDN'T YOU TELL ME my father was up there?"

Ms. Hanover looks at me. "I was hoping you'd notice him yourself."

I look up at my dad and smile. *Stop looking down — you're missing all the good stuff.*

Fred compares my face — the painting — and the photograph. "Spitting image!" he says.

The Champ's jaw, resting on his chest, rises up and down with each breath. He's still asleep, but he's softly grunting and bobbing his head as if dodging punches.

"Time to go," says Ms. Hanover.

Fred is already out the front door hailing us a cab.

Ms. Hanover walks to the front window and slips her hands into her jeans pockets. She turns her head and looks up and down the street. Behind her, the barroom is noisy with clinking glasses, coughing, and cheering a Thurman Munson double off the wall.

I walk over and stand beside her — the Champ's paintings rolled up, tucked safely under my arm. "Ms. Hanover, the Champ had a son."

She nods. "Yes. Luke."

"Did he die?"

"Ben didn't talk about him much. He died in Spain; a car crash."

"When did he die?"

"At the end of his boxing career, I think."

When he adopted Lavender.

"Ms. Hanover, why did the Champ leave his son?"

She tilts her head and starts braiding her long black hair while looking out the window. Suddenly, she slips into a Chinese accent. "Well...Once upon a time there was this high fence in China, and it separated two lands. One side was sad, the other side was happy. You with me?"

"So far." I nod. "But why the Chinese accent?"

"I'm Confucius," she says, bowing politely. "One day a brave young man living on the sad side scaled to the top and hopped down onto the happy side. You know what he did next?"

"No."

"He waved good-bye and disappeared."

"Selfish," I say.

"Ah! Not so fast, *xue sheng*," says Confucius, raising his finger. "The very next day, another brave young man hopped atop the same fence, straddled it, and helped other people climb over so they could live on the happy side." Confucius turns his palms upward and motions as if weighing something. "So, *xue sheng*, who's the better man?"

"Easy—the second one."

"I, Confucius, contend both men are equally good. One helps by leading. The other helps by assisting."

I shift Barlow's paintings to my other arm. "Ms. Hanover, I asked why Barlow left his son. Why the story?"

"You don't see the connection? Some fathers are leaders and some are helpers. Sailor Barlow—maybe even your father—is a leader. Me, a teacher, I'm a helper."

I look back at the Champ snoring. I begin to see him differently. "The Champ was selfish."

"You have a point. But he might never have become Sailor Barlow. His picture, or your father's picture, might not be hanging up on the Blarney Stone walls if they didn't do what they did."

"Ignore us?"

"Not as simple as that."

"Barlow's son needed him."

"And you need your father," she says softly.

I look up at my father sitting at the piano.

"Perhaps fathers help their children in other ways," she says.

I look at the Champ sleeping, his mouth hanging open.

"It sounds harsh," she says, "but checkbook-love is better than no love."

I look at Ms. Hanover.

She puts her hand on my shoulder and shakes her head sympathetically. "Money is never enough."

I look at the reflection of myself in the dirty window.

"You don't have to agree with Confucius," she says, "just understand his parable."

I understand his damn parable. It sucks.

Chapter 45

MS. HANOVER KEEPS STARING OUT the front window, thinking. She's running her fingers through her long black hair—she sure has alotta hair, probably a yards worth—and not one gray strand. She's just standing here in deep thought, chewing the inside of her cheek.

"Parables are imperfect," she finally says, "just like the people who create them. Too many kids grow up without leaders or helpers. Kids need to work through it and move on. Ultimately—and this is the hard part—kids must forgive their parents."

"Just suck it up?" I say.

She nods and scratches her tattoo.

"How about your parents?" I ask.

"What about them?"

"Did you get along?"

"There were rough patches."

"What did your parents do for a living?"

"Mother stayed home. Father was an English teacher."

"The apple doesn't fall too far from the tree, huh?"

She smiles. "Not exactly. I'm adopted."

"Oh, sorry."

She shrugs and continues looking out the window, left and right.

"How about your real dad?" I ask.

"My adopted dad is my real dad."

"Ever know your—"

"Biological mother and father?"

I nod. "I mean, didn't you ever get angry because they—?"

"I worked through it. They were parents only in a scientific way."

Was she an unwanted boarder baby from China? Ever since Wanda planted boarder babies in my brain, I can't shake it. It isn't something I'd ever ask a teacher because it's none of my business.

"Ms. Hanover, were you a boarder baby?"

She chuckles. I hope she isn't mad at me for asking such a personal question, but she suddenly turns and walks away, with her long black horsetail swishing behind her. She begins helping the bartender pour shots.

Confucius is wrong. My father and Barlow are just plain selfish.

I look over and listen to the Champ burbling little snores. My jackass stepfather also snores, but he's clever about it, claiming he sleeps with enthusiasm. Suddenly, a horrible thought hits me: *I'm a boarder baby!* I board in my stepfather's house. He's bribed my mother with expensive gifts and long vacations. My mother loves being pampered. It's disgusting. Why am I always so polite to him when all I want to do is scream "I hate your guts!"

Suck it up, just like Ms. Hanover says.

She walks back to the front window, and continues looking left and right.

"Looking for someone?" I ask.

"Just checking."

"You're looking for my father, aren't you?"

"No. Your cab."

Something tells me she's lying—it's something about her smile. But I let it slide.

Maybe she's looking for her biological father and mother?

She points with her chin. "Here it is."

I turn to wake the Champ, but he's gone. The booth is empty.

"I thought you were watching him," she says.

We search the room and then the restrooms.

No Barlow!

Chapter 46

THE CHAMP IS IN THE kitchen—his head's inside a trash can, and he's grabbing table scraps for Lavender.

"Dog needs food," he says, holding a plastic bag full of table scraps. It's pathetic, but touching, how devoted the Champ is to Lavender. I personally think it's psychological, the way he's bonded with a dog after losing his son.

"We'll feed her later," I say, showing him the dog leash, as if that means anything.

The Champ smiles. "You're a good son, Luke."

"What took so long?" snaps Fred, sitting in the Yellow Checker cab.

I tell him about the Champ digging into a garbage can. Quietly, I explain about Champ's moments of clarity, and right now wasn't one of them. "He roams at night, so he's tethered to his bed," I whisper.

Fred shakes his head and points to the buried treasure tucked under my arm. "I just don't understand it."

It's nighttime on Third Avenue, and the neon lights—yellows, greens, blues, and reds—look real pretty. I turn to Fred. "So, you know my dad, huh?"

"Yeah."

"How?"

"He comes in to eat."

"A lot?"

He shrugs. "Enough. Watches the Yanks."

"And drink a few beers?"

He nods.

The cab stops at a red light.

"Nice man, your father. Humble. Sensitive."

"Ms. Hanover knew he was my dad all along," I say. "She shoulda told me."

He looks at me and then out the window.

"She's a liar," I say.

"Isn't everybody?" he grins.

"She said she hates bums. But that's a lie."

Fred shakes his head. "She hates their laziness, and fear, and chip-on-the-shoulder attitudes which land them down here in the first place."

The cabbie beeps his horn, cursing a bicyclist veering in front of him.

"Professor Ping's got little tolerance for the shit mentality that chains people to their misery. Sometimes people invite their own mental illness, you know."

Is he talking about my dad? Or me?

I turn my head and continue looking out the window at the dark summer night, the red lights, honking cars, and people rushing to God knows where.

"Bad habits die hard," he says, "but people can change."

I think of my own bad habits. I mash my nose hard against the window. I clench my fists, and dig my fingernails into my palms. "I see all that shit in me too," I say softly.

Fred places his hand on my thigh. "Matt, we're all scared little bunny rabbits underneath it all."

For some reason I feel like crying, right here in the cab, but I suck back the tears.

"Don't be so hard on yourself," he whispers, "or on your father."

The biggest truth is I'm not hard enough on myself. I haven't accomplished a damn thing in three years. I'm seventeen and already life's passing me by. I mash my nose harder against the window and gouge my fingernails deeper into my palms.

I'm sick of myself.

Fuck it! From this day on, all the fear, anger, and hate squirming inside me, polluting me, will be channeled. Football's starting in a few weeks, and I'm gonna sprint so hard my legs will puke. Coach Sgro is gonna love me again. That's a fact.

Fred pokes me with his elbow. "Know what I like about you, Matt?"

"What?"

"Your honesty. You're only as sick as your secrets."

After a short ride, our cab pulls to the curb, and the Champ and I step out. Fred lowers his window and motions me closer. "Your father chose an extremely difficult road, but he's one hellava musician. Don't ever lose sight of that."

"Thank you."

"Here, take my business card," he says, fumbling for his wallet. He pulls out a card, but it drops to the floor of the cab. He bends down, picks it up, and hands it to me. "Call me if you need advice with Barlow's paintings."

The cab pulls away.

"C'mon, Champ," I say, looking over my shoulder. I stick out my hand for him to hold — but he's gone. "Champ! Champ?"

He's gone!

I clutch his paintings to my chest and race up the block, poking my head inside an off-track betting office. "Champ!" People stare at me like I'm nuts.

I run in the opposite direction. "Champ! Champ!"

He can't have gone too far.

I run down one side of the street, then up the other. Where is he? It's late and I need to get him back to the hospital. But first I had to find him!

On the opposite corner, I spot him kneeling down, petting a lady's white terrier.

Dodging honking traffic, I run toward them. "I'm sorry, ma'am," I say, catching my breath. "Hope he didn't frighten you. He shouldn't be running off like that. He's a bit confused this evening."

She smiles. "It's okay. I could see he was a dog lover. Besides, I thought I recognized his face from somewhere."

I want to explain to this lady that this battle-scarred man is the great Benny "Sailor" Barlow, the former light heavyweight champion of the world, and I am his lucky son.

But it's late and we gotta get back to the hospital.

Chapter 47

ICAN'T WAIT TO TELL Mr. Karp about my discovery as the Champ and I walk down 14th Street toward the subway to go cross town. "Champ, you're gonna make your comeback!"

Just like Fred said, the Bowery is undergoing a massive face-lift with fancy restaurants with frilly curtains, chic clothing boutiques, and trendy health spas, if you like that sort of thing. Newness is popping up on both sides of the street—a Vietnamese restaurant, a posh health spa. It's a tug-of-war between new and old, and it's easy to get lost in the newness.

"Hold my hand," I say.

The Champ refuses.

I stop walking and pull out Mimi's dog leash that's rolled up in my pocket.

"Hold this, then," I say.

"No."

"C'mon, Dad--hold it."

"Why?"

"'Cause you're tired."

"Ain't."

"You're beginning to stumble."

He shrugs and his hand reaches for the leash. *At least I'm connected to something*, says a distant voice, as we walk down into the subway.

We're a pair of mismatched boxing gloves. But we are connected — like father and son. I drop in two subway tokens and we walk through the turnstile.

Behind us I hear trouble. This always happens when things are going good.

A pack of loud teenagers, badly in need of haircuts and wearing the young felon look, are loping down the stairs. Their baseball caps are twisted backward, and cigarettes are wedged behind their ears. They jump the turnstile.

These guys don't look too friendly, but the biggest kid is smiling. "Got a dollar?" he says.

I shake my head. "Not for you."

My response is pretty funny because they all start laughing.

He walks closer. "Wanna fight me, douchebag?"

"No," I say, "but if you get any closer I'll gladly piss on your leg." It wasn't the smartest thing to say.

He reaches out to grab the canvases. I smack his hand away.

The Champ notices and walks toward us. When the punk gets a closer look at Barlow's battered face, it gives him pause. It's a dangerous face.

"Whoa, old man! How many car accidents you been in?"

The Champ steps closer and snarls. Then he lifts his gnarled fist up to the punk's pus to get his attention. "Wanna hit me?" he mutters.

The punk laughs, but fear's leaking out of him. "Nah, old man, jus' playin' wit'cha."

"Get outta here," snarls the Champ.

Which they do.

"Annoying, weren't they?" he says.

Chapter 48

IT'S HOT AND HUMID DOWN here in the subway, and the Champ shuffles forward, bends over, and shuts his eyes. He groans and drops Lavender's bag of food to the floor. He begins rubbing his temples like he has a headache.

"You okay?"

He shakes his head, and his words are slow and careful. "Can't pretend no more…You ain't Luke."

I keep my mouth shut. There's nothing to be gained by opening it.

His shoulders slump. "Died in a car crash…Dog's prob'ly dead too."

I nod.

He looks down at the bag of scraps, gently kicks it with his toe. "You lied to me, kid."

I look at his sad face. I feel bad — real bad. Everything must have, all of a sudden, clicked. I guess this is a moment of clarity.

He lifts his head, squares his shoulders, and says, "Go…hospital."

We start walking down the steps to catch the L train. How am I gonna explain his absence? I need to think of something real quick. God put a brain in me for a purpose, but I don't have a damn clue.

We leave Lavender's food on the floor.

Soft piano music is drifting up from below. Music always makes the drab subway less drabby. All over town, musicians perform on subway platforms. Singers sing, drummers drum, and flutists flute. This musician is playing my dad's song "Harlequinade." Its tempo is hummingbird fast, full of trills and grace notes. Whoever is playing it is playing nice and slow.

The Champ starts humming the tune.

"You know this song?"

"Know the guy who wrote it."

I stop in my tracks. "You do?"

"George Watt."

"How do you know George Watt?"

"Lived in Sunshine…across the hall."

My father was living in a flophouse?

"He's my f-father," I say.

The Champ looks at me. "Yeah, look like 'im…That's pro'ly him playin'."

That's just plain stupid.

Could it be my father?

We walk down the concrete steps toward the music.

I hold onto the stair-railing, trying to catch my breath, and my knees are spongy and weak. It's The Unthinkable…His face is skinny and gray, and the slow music leaking out of him is so damn heartbreaking. His hair is long and stringy, his shirt is clean-ish.

The air is dank and suffocating, but people are nodding their heads and swaying their bodies as his thin fingers play the slow ballad. A basket of change and crumpled bills is under his keyboard. His black shoes are worn.

His spotlight is now the dingy lightbulbs of the subway. My dad's a panhandler.

What would my mother say?

Thank God he doesn't notice me; it's been two years. Would he recognize his own shirt, pants, and shoes that the Champ is wearing?

After finishing his song, he looks up and wipes his whiskered face with a handkerchief. When he spots me standing on the stairs, his jaw drops. Within seconds I'm in his embrace. I hold on to his shoulders to steady myself. I'm crying big, for sure. I don't mind crying because crying brings you closer to that person.

I found my lost father!

After he kisses me a few million times, he wipes his eyes dry, he says, "You want to know why am I down here, right?"

I don't know what to say. His tie is loosened and his sweaty shirt is sticking to his back.

"Well, I was going to ask you the same question."

I'm speechless. His face is deeply lined and his eyes are sunken in their sockets.

"I'm sorry you're seeing me like this," he says, combing his long hair with his fingers. "And I'm sorry for this past year."

"Two," I say.

"But I never forgot you," he says. "I always sent money." He shakes his head. "That's no excuse, I know, but after…Daniel and the divorce…" He shakes his head again and looks away. That's when he sees the Champ standing beside me. "Hello, Benny."

The Champ nods. "George."

"Been awhile."

"Has."

"You okay?"

"Yeah. You?"

I look at my dad's tired face. He's got that sunken-cheek look, like Hackensack Mack. "Dad, you don't look too good."

"Difficult year…." His hollow eyes look far away. "It was horrible seeing him like that. Your mother and I loved him so much."

It's terrible seeing my dad still replaying Daniel's death.

"Danny was always a handful," I say softly. I close my eyes and replay a memory. Danny's in the backyard screaming at me, "Get Dad!" I run and find our father in the piano room. Dad and I are running to the backyard and see Daniel's friend, Joseph, hanging by his neck up in a tree. Daniel starts laughing because it's all a joke. He has rigged a safety harness under Joseph's shirt.

Another Daniel memory: A few years earlier, Daniel and his three friends are at the Jersey Shore digging a deep hole in the sand. They're throwing me in the hole and burying me up to my neck. They are dumping a metal sand bucket over my head and walking away laughing. I'm yelling for help until a lifeguard rescues me. Big joke.

My dad says, "We have a lot to talk about. Let's go someplace nice."

When we get up to go, I start to explain about the Champ and his paintings, but he's gone.

Again!

Chapter 49

LIFE'S STUPID CRAZY! IT TAKES two years to find my dad, but a split second to lose the Champ. We search everywhere. At least he's not lying dead on the third rail. We finally find a cop on 14th Street and tell him about the Champ.

"Sailor Barlow?" he says. "Ain't that the horse puncher, the guy that killed a guy in the ring?"

Our cabby drives me and my dad uptown. He cuts over to 23rd Street, hangs an illegal left on 42nd Street, then another on Eighth.

"Where we going?" I ask.

"A restaurant—your mother's favorite."

"But I'm worried about the Champ."

"Don't be," says dad. "Someone'll see the tag around his wrist and return him."

The cabbie circles around Columbus Circle, and then hits Lincoln Center where we get out. This is upper-class territory—no pawn shops, check-cashing joint or Blarney Stones.

The maître'd, wearing a crisp tuxedo, looks surprised when we enter the restaurant. "George, tonight's your night off," he says.

"Miguel, I want you to meet *un persona muy importante.*"

Miguel looks at me and smiles. "Your son! A remarkable likeness! *Su padre* talk about you all the time." He grabs my dad's keyboard, checks it into a closet, and comes back holding two dinner jackets. He then escorts us to a corner table, beside a white grand piano.

I can see my mother really liking this joint. She's all about elegance and good taste. Everything here is dainty, prim, and proper. It's marble columns and pink tablecloths. The wallpaper isn't even wallpaper — it's textured cloth. One wall is mirrored, giving it the illusion of much more space than there really is. The gross amount of elegance makes my teeth ache.

I lay the Champ's canvases on the pink tablecloth.

A waiter walks over. "Something to drink, George?"

"Coke," I say.

"The usual," says my dad.

The waiter hurries off.

"The usual?"

"Seltzer with a twist of lemon." Dad's red eyes sweep through the dining room. "Your mother adored this place," he says. "She relished the excitement of rubbing elbows with the elite."

I nod.

"Your mother is a beautiful person herself, you know."

"Why did you bring me here?" I ask.

He points to the piano. "I work here."

"Playing piano?"

He nods. "But that's not the main reason."

I look at a face that has changed — and not for the better.

"This is where your mother and I first met...And the place we finally said good-bye. May fifteenth."

The waiter returns with our drinks and sets them on the table. Dad lifts his glass. "A toast to my wonderful son." He takes a healthy gulp.

I unfold my pink napkin and place it on my left thigh. My father notices my impeccable etiquette and smiles. "That's your mother's influence. She knows Emily Post like the back of her hand."

True. Proper table manners are high on my mother's list of things to master: how to drink soup (spoon moves away from you), how to cut meat (one piece at a time), and elbows must never touch the table. She wouldn't approve of the dirt under my father's fingernails.

He gently places his glass back on the table. "I still love your mother, you know," he says, looking around the room. "This is what your mother wanted. I tried to give it to her, but couldn't." He then leans back in his chair and tells me about May fifteenth their last night together.

"A piano player?" my mother said. "I can't be married to a piano player, for God's sake."

"I need to make a living," my father replied.

"How much can a piano player make?"

"Enough. And we still have my royalties coming in."

"Okay, but a piano player?"

"Yes."

"What's wrong with you?"

"I don't know," my dad said. "Daniel…"

"I'm grieving too. You don't think I'm grieving, too? I was his mother."

"I know you are...were."

"So, you're not going to write music anymore?"

"I'm tired. It's a different type of music today, honey."

My mother glared at him, and as she glared, he could see her slowly detach from him.

"My God, don't do it," she said.

"Why not?"

"Because I married a talented musician, not a piano player."

"We love each other," he said, reaching across the table to hold her hand. "Don't we?"

She leaned back. "I'll divorce you."

"Leave me?"

"A piano player?" She slowly shook her head "You're better than that."

"You would leave me?"

"One minute I'm living in a nice house with two lovely sons and a talented composer, the man who's going to be the next Oscar Hammerstein"--my father looked into his lap--"and the next minute I'm living in a cheap house in New Jersey with one son and a drunk who's a common piano player."

"Won't exactly be like that," said my dad.

"It's too humiliating. I wasn't brought up for something like this. I can't do that."

"Maybe I can write jingles," said my dad. "That pays decent."

"That's so off the wall," my mother said. "I can't wait for you to get your act together or reinvent yourself with jingles. Where will I end up? Last year's beauty queen? This year's charwoman?"

"You don't love me," my father said.

My mother looked away. She took in a deep breath and looked back at him. She seemed as if she might cry. But she didn't.

"You don't love me," repeated my dad.

"Not enough," she said.

I look at my dad's sunken cheeks. "Dad, I think we've all been escaping — you, me, mom, and Daniel."

His face goes blank.

"Daniel found his escape, then you. My mother is escaping to Europe."

He nods.

"I've been escaping too," I say.

You're only as sick as your secrets.

Chapter 50

"Matt, I've lost myself," says my dad. "I'm out of tune—please forgive me." His eyes are moist as he dabs tears away with his pink napkin. I look at his dirty fingernails. He isn't like the leader in a Confucius parable. He looks down into his lap.

"Daniel, Daniel, Daniel. After he died, I sometimes felt like…killing myself," he says softly.

"Dad!"

"Yeah, I was lucky and had a few hit songs. I'm either a successful failure or a failed success—but I am a has-been." He shakes his head. "Sometimes I still see myself ending it all. Jumping off the Brooklyn Bridge."

"Dad, stop!" I'm a seventeen-year-old tough guy, but I'm feeling like a little kid. It's just too terrible to think about my father jumping off a bridge.

He takes another gulp of his seltzer and gently sets it down on the table. "I thought about moving to California, there's work there, but I couldn't. I wouldn't. I want to be close to you."

"But you left me, Dad! You never came on weekends!"

"I'm sorry."

"I waited for you. Every weekend. I thought you'd show up."

"I know. I took a year off."

"Two."

"I'm sorry. I'll make it up to you."

I lean across the table. "You told me your father left you. Now you're doing it to me."

He reaches for my hand. "I'll never leave you, son."

I want to believe him so much.

He smiles. "This weekend let's have a picnic in Central Park. I'll bring the sandwiches and drinks. Okay?"

"Okay."

I so much want to believe him.

I stand up and walk to the bathroom because, well, these intimate conversations suck. And this one really sucks. I hope he can muscle through his depression or whatever it is and get back on track. When I return, he says he's sorry, again and again and again.

"When's your mother coming back?" he asks.

I shrug.

"Where is she?"

"Somewhere in Europe."

He tilts his head. "Somewhere?"

"She sends postcards."

"She's been gone a long time."

"Nine months."

He takes a sip from his glass. He looks concerned.

"Dad," I say, "ever since she divorced you, I've divorced her."

He looks at the piano and gives that some thought.

Then we get talking about the Champ's brain damage and his paintings and his secret hiding spot inside the kitchen table. I tell him about Ms. Hanover and Funny Fred at the Blarney Stone. I tell him about Wanda and Dr. Roth. And I share with him my plan of bringing the Champ back into the limelight with November's art show.

But there's still one more critical—secret—step to my plan.

"What's this critical, secret step?" he asks.

I shake my head. I won't tell anybody. Until it happens.

"Well," he nods, "I'm very proud of you. You've managed to keep busy—and keep your nose clean?"

I nod. He doesn't need to know about my fighting, failing, stealing, and lying.

"And I met a friend. You'd like her."

"Her?"

"Mimi Breedlove. She helped me find these paintings."

He nods. "So you discovered twenty-one valuable paintings?" he says, tapping them with his index finger. "May I see one?"

I carefully unroll them and hand him the topmost canvas. He stares at it for a long time. He puts his hand to his mouth. "My goodness!"

"That man," I say pointing, "is a great songwriter. He's a bit out of tune, but he'll be making a comeback soon. And he's the best dad a kid could ever have."

He stands, walks around the table, and hugs me.

At the end of the night he hails a Yellow cab and tells the driver to chauffer me back home to New Jersey. Dad digs into his hip pocket, pulls out a few bills and presses them into my palm. "We'll be in touch," he says.

I want to believe him so much. I look at his sunken cheeks and dirty fingernails.

His breath doesn't smell of seltzer with a twist of lemon.

Chapter 51

I<small>T'S THE LAST WEEK OF</small> August and Ivan Karp, still wearing his Detroit Tigers cap, is carefully inspecting twenty new Benny Barlow originals that Mimi and I have carefully laid out on the gallery floor for him.

Ivan Karp, bending down, chuckles. "Hidden inside a kitchen table?"

I nod. "In a sunken compartment."

"Utterly fantastic!" he laughs.

"Primitive art isn't supposed to be sophisticated," he says, "but this stuff is...absolutely delicious and graceful." He crouches down to examine a landscape. Kneeling beside him are two young assistants, one holding a yardstick, the other writing down measurements.

"Ingrid," says Karp, "you notice the delicate flecks of sunlight here?"

Ingrid nods. "I like the shadowing of that city scene," she says, pointing.

"Ivan," says the guy assistant, "you see these fight scenes? Fucking brutal!"

Karp looks at each painting. "Egad! A subtle primitive! Who woulda thunk it? Intelligent yet romantic; concrete yet mysterious—and a hell of a prizefighter."

Mimi and I are sitting in Karp's office, in the same hardback chairs as before. He's sitting behind his cluttered desk.

"So, does Mr. Barlow get his show?" I ask.

He hands us a contract. "You're on for November. Barlow needs to sign it. Get it back to me tomorrow."

Mimi examines the document—even though she never saw one in her life.

"This show's gonna be eye-popping," he says, adjusting his cap.

"A knockout!" I say, smiling.

"You know, a year ago Muhammad Ali's twelve dinky ink sketches sold out in a day, and they were mere doodles." Karp then shakes his head and chuckles. "Hidden treasure inside a table!"

"And a dirty seat cushion, don't forget that," adds Mimi, looking up from the contract.

"Don't worry, little lady, I didn't forget you."

She smiles and says, "I know you don't mean to be sexist, Mr. Karp."

Karp rolls his eyes. "Accept my sincerest apologies, deary."

"Accepted," she says, going back to the contract. "I'm sure it won't happen again."

Mr. Karp grins and reaches into his top desk drawer, pulls out a thin cigar, unwraps it, and sticks it into his mouth. "What a fantastic story! No one's gonna believe it. Sailor Barlow's paintings, lost and found!"

"Just like himself," I say.

"Oh?" he looks at me.

"At first, he didn't even remember he was a world champion."

"He didn't?"

"He's damaged."

"Sad…very sad," says Karp, shaking his head and rotating his cigar with his fingers. He looks up at the ceiling, probably remembering a young Sailor Barlow battling in the ring.

This is the perfect time to pitch the crucial part of my secret plan—the most important part.

"Hey, Mr. Karp, do you know that TV show *Lost Stars: Where Are They Now?*"

"Sure. NBC."

"Think they'd be interested in doing a show on the Champ here at your gallery?"

His face is blank. Then lights up. "Tape an episode of *Lost Stars* here—at my gallery?"

I nod my head. "Sure, why not?"

He sits back, thinks about it, and then laughs. "That's so fucking genius! Let me contact some people!" He quickly grabs the telephone and starts dialing. "A seat cushion! A kitchen table! No one'll fuckin' believe it!"

Mimi turns her head to me and grins.
I just hit a grand slam homerun!

Chapter 52

WHEN I GET HOME, GRAM is sitting in the den watching *Jeopardy*. She looks up when I enter the room. "You win your game?" I bend down and kiss her forehead. "Yeah, and I hit a moonshot!"

"Congratulations, Mr. Mantle! When you finish patting yourself on the back, dinner's waiting for you on the stove and there's a postcard on the kitchen table."

This one's from Italy with a colorful photo of the Roman Coliseum.

Dear Matthew,

> *I'm sorry our stay in Europe has kept us apart for so long, but Jack's program is a tremendous hit — much more than anticipated.*
> *I pray you will bury your anger and forgive us. This trip is crucial for us all and will work out in the end — I promise. Please understand, this vacation has been good for me. I have needed the rest. Your grandmother says you've made a complete turnaround. I am also pleased to learn about your B+ in summer school. I miss you and love you so much! I can't wait to hold you in my arms upon our return!*

Love and kisses,
Mom

"Hey, Gram," I shout from the kitchen, "Does Italy get *Lost Stars — Where Are They Now?*"

Chapter 53

THE AIR IS SOFT AND fresh and the bright blue sky stretches all the way to Arkansas. It's the day before school, and Mimi and I are curled up on The Hump, the part that's flat like a bed. A pink cotton-candy blanket with satin edging is spread beneath us—the blanket is Mimi's idea.

"Howdy, cowboy," she whispers into my ear. She's wearing gold hoop earrings and a bit of eyeshadow. Her glossy pink lips are parted and her teeth are perfectly white. It's sure nice being so close. As I stroke her short black hair, which has sprouted up another half inch, I tell her about meeting my dad, our Central Park picnic, and then about our row-boating on the lake, but I suddenly bolt up. "Oops! Sorry. I'll shut up."

"What's wrong?" she says.

"I'm so goddamned self-centered!"

"What?"

"I'm talking about me instead of asking about you. That's not being valiant." I've been waiting a long time to use that new word.

She smiles and yanks me down by my shoulders. "You're so adorable." Then she nestles her head onto my chest.

"Let's start again," I say. "How's your father?"

She's lying on her side with her head propped up with her hand. "Well, Mr. Valiant, as you know, it's been the summer from hell for our family. I mean, doctors tried every remedy known to man. One doctor even tried veterinary medicines intended to deworm horses."

"Gross!" I'm very eloquent.

"They even tried industrial insecticides. I'd tell you the names, but they're too long and complicated."

"Is he okay?"

"Wait, I'm not finished. What happened is this—a friend of a friend of a friend read an article in, of all places, *Popular Mechanics,* about a dermatologist who treated Morgellons patients by putting a cast over the lesions. So we tried it, and after one week my dad's lesions were healed."

"On his face?"

She smiles. "They punched out nose holes and a big opening for his mouth. Poor Daddy looked like The Mummy! He stayed home, drank chicken broth through a straw, and sat on the couch for a week watching *Bonanza* and Walter Cronkite."

"That sucks," I say. I was on a roll.

"You said it! Especially nasty microbes that burrow into your father's body, eat his flesh, and threaten his livelihood."

She gently brushes off a black ant crawling onto her white short-shorts. Her fingernails, I notice, are no longer bitten red-raw. "So, how's Sailor Barlow?" she asks.

I clasp my hands behind my head and look up into the apple tree. "Dr. Roth moved him to an after-care facility in South Jersey. Wanda and I are visiting him once he settles in."

She hugs me. "You found his buried treasure, Matt."

I nod and begin describing the Champ's twenty-one paintings in detail—his farm scenes with grazing horses, European landscapes, city scenes, portraits, and, of course, his boxing paintings. And I don't stutter once.

"I don't think I've ever heard so many words fly out of your mouth at once. I mean, isn't it against your brooding male nature to talk so much?"

I smile. I'm talking a bunch because I'm excited for the Champ's upcoming rebirth.

She kisses my forehead and whispers, "You're The Wonderful Matt Watt."

"You're The Valiant Mimi Breedlove," I say, evening it out.

We lay here quietly curled up on her pink blanket. I gently rub the small of her back and look at her cute little ears. How can ears be sexy? She closes her eyes and purrs. Her smile is warm and catlike. I smell her coconut shampoo.

I'm in love.

Suddenly, she props herself up on her elbow again and looks at me. Her smile is gone and her face is full of concern.

"What?" I say.

"I'm afraid."

Chapter 54

"WHY ARE YOU AFRAID?" I ask.

"Because you hate your mother."

"Because I hate my mother?" I say, sitting up.

"Yes. Why do you hate your mother?"

"Don't hate her."

"Do too," she says. "It's obvious, Matt. You hate your mother."

"Come off it," I scoff.

She looks directly into my eyes. "We're friends, right?"

"Yeah, so?"

She reaches out for my hand and places it on her breast. "But we're friends who want to…be more." She looks into her lap and bites her lower lip.

"More?"

She tilts her head flirtatiously and begins to blush. "You know what I mean."

It's fascinating to watch the blush spread over her pretty face. I know exactly what she means, and I begin nervously chewing the inside of my cheek.

"Matt, we're friends, but we're friends who want to… you know…"

I feel a stiffening in my jeans. The urge to merge?

"But," she adds, "it's impossible to get emotionally close with each other if, you know, you're not emotionally close to your mother."

I look at her beautiful blushing face.

"I don't know if you *can* love me," she says, removing my hand.

I just look at her. I always mess things up at the end. I turn my head and spit.

"Matt!" she announces, "stay with me — this is an adult conversation."

I grin. "Oh, good. I always wanted to have one of those."

"I'm not joking, Matthew. You're seventeen. It's time you fixed your relationship with your mom." Her blush has faded, and I look into the woods.

"I love my mother," I say, "but I hate her more." The words just walk out my mouth.

"You need to fix that."

I look down at the crack on the side of The Hump, where water is still leaking. This time I get the feeling it's cleaning itself, not crying.

"Mimi, I agree. My mother is an important part of my life, and because she's my mother I'm supposed to love her. But I can raise myself, thank you. Besides, haven't you ever loved someone without liking them very much?"

Mimi continues looking at me with concern. "Matthew, girlfriends and mothers are connected, if you didn't know. My father once told me there's only one woman — your mother — and there's a million versions of her. If you don't love her, you probably can't love a girlfriend. That's just how it works."

Her words are very impactful and the importance of connections suddenly hits — just like Sailor Barlow punching me in the hospital.

Everything's connected!

Mimi and me is a connection. Mimi's father has been cured by a friend of a friend of a friend — those were connections. The dog-man leashed to a woman is a connection. Sailor Barlow wanting to get punched is a connection. I'm connected to boxing royalty. OK Harris Art Gallery connected with *Lost Stars.* I look up into the tree: branches, leaves, roots, earth, apples.

My grandmother was right. Ever since my brother died and my parents divorced, my heart has squeezed shut like a fist, not wanting to make connections. But with Mimi, I've allowed myself to spill my guts and she spilled her guts and now we're best friends. My grandmother is right: "Shared joy is double joy. Shared sorrow is half sorrow."

Connection is not a dog leash around my neck — connection is a reassuring hug around my heart.

Suddenly, I get a brand-new dazzling idea. It's like the sun shining inside my head. "Mimi, you have it backwards. If I love you, I'll learn to love my mother!"

She grins. "Nice try, cowboy."

I look up into the tree and think about my mother. Do I love her without liking her?

Mimi and I, lying side by side, look up through the branches and listen to the forest singing — the birds and the leaves blowing in the warm September breeze. She rests her head on my shoulder, and she gazes into my eyes. I am connected.

"Mimi, would it be okay if I kiss you?"

"You mean now?" She grins.

I'm a tough guy, but I feel nervous — just a little bittish. So I do the most obvious thing — tickle her. I get on my knees, lean over, and go for her sides. She starts laughing like crazy and kicks me away — right off The Hump. Thump! I'm lying on my back with dead leaves twisted in my hair. I spit dirt from my mouth and look up at her laughing face.

"Who're you laughing at?" I shout.

"YOU!"

Then she starts singing:

"Humpty Dumpty sat on a wall. Humpty Dumpty had a great fall — "

"Shut up!"

"All the king's horses, and all the king's men couldn't put Humpy together again."

My cheeks are on fire. Deep down in my gut, anger, shame, disappointment, and resentment explode. Suddenly, everything makes perfect fucking sense! Me, my father, Sailor Barlow are weak men damaged by life! We are three Humpty Dumptys! We're losers! The truth is so fucking bitter, painful, and familiar. "Shut up!" I bellow.

"Make me, loser!" she teases.

I scramble up the rock, and, sort of, pounce on top of her. I yank her arms over her head and pin her tiny wrists together. Then I start tickling the shit outta her with my free hand.

"Lemme go!" But there's real excitement in her laughter.

I keep tickling. My teeth clench, my jaw is tight with anger and shame.

"You're being mean!" she squeals. She wraps her legs around my waist and wiggles to get free, but her wiggle isn't much of a wiggle,

194

and she's smiling from ear to ear, and if that doesn't say consent, I don't know what does.

So I tickle harder.

"This isn't funny!" she laughs.

"I'm enjoying it!"

"Big tough guy can tickle a girl half his size."

"Isn't hard." By then, my anger's drained out and my face relaxes. Somehow, I feel clean…and relaxed.

After catching her breath, she narrows her eyes. "So, tough guy, what else can you do to me?" I realize I'm supposed to do something more to her. If she was a guy, I'd know exactly what I'd do. I'd hold her down and drop one long disgusting string of spit and suck it back up at the very last second before it dropped on her face.

But that's not what I do.

I bend my head down and kiss her open mouth.

Let's leave it at that.

Chapter 55

No less than five television vans are parked outside of The OK Harris Gallery. The gallery is a renovated warehouse located at 383 West Broadway, and is considered the heartbeat of contemporary art in New York City. Mimi and I walk up the three black cast-iron steps, where a doorman wearing a snazzy red jacket with important gold buttons holds the door open. I hobble inside.

The gallery is hopping! Bright TV lights and camera crews are clustered throughout the gallery, and people, sipping champagne from plastic glasses, are pointing at the Champ's framed paintings hanging on the walls. A large crowd is pressed close to a huge TV screen watching one of the Champ's championship fights. *"A left and a right and Walcott's down! Barlow's in total command, punching hard…"*

I'm hobbling because of a painful blister from my wet football cleats. This year I'm the starting varsity halfback and Coach Sgro loves me again, but no one's bragging.

Mimi and I pull off our winter coats and stand in line to get them checked. The line is busy with art critics, art collectors, and a lot of businessy-looking people.

Mimi does a quick one-two with her lipstick and whispers, "Is my hair a mess?"

"Kinda," I say.

She pinches my arm. "You could've told me earlier."

"Mimi," I say, hooking my arm through hers, "you look exquisite."

I've waited a long time to use that word, too.

She looks around the gallery and smiles. "Mr. Barlow's making his comeback tonight — thanks to The Wonderful Matthew Watt!"

"And The Magnificent Mimi Breedlove."

She kicks my shin. "I like magical better."

"The Magnificently Magical Mimi Breedlove," I whisper.

She stands on her tiptoes and kisses me.

Mimi and I are officially going steady. And she really does look exquisitely funky, wearing her pink-green-black-orange peasant dress with pink platform sneakers. Another reason I'm feeling good is because the Champ's comeback is being aired on national television!

After fixing her hair, Mimi flips open tonight's glossy brochure and begins reading. "Hey, look! It says there are twenty-two paintings."

I look where she points and shake my head. "Typo." Typo or not, tonight promises to be a knockout. "Too bad the Champ's not here."

"He is here!" Mimi points to his paintings. "He's in that golden field, and in that Spanish church, and in that ring. And your father's here too, playing piano."

I nod. "Yeah." My blister's killing me.

I've been searching for my dad since entering the gallery — but it's Dr. Roth, sipping champagne, I see. He's wearing a white Oxford shirt, blue blazer, and well-creased khakis. And he's slicked back his thick hair with extra mousse. He stands there concentrating on a farmer grooming a white horse. When he turns and sees me, he walks over and shakes my hand. "Congratulations, Matthew! This show's outstanding. It's certain to meet with critical approval."

I nod.

"Tonight," he says, "is undoubtedly one of the most exciting openings I've attended in years. The lush colors, the pulsing energy oozing off these canvases — it's all here."

I look at the lush colors and pulsing energy oozing off the canvases. Then I look at the pulsing energy of the reporters and camera crews running around.

The doctor turns to Mimi. "Is this your lady friend? She's pretty as a picture!"

"And smart, too," she says.

He raises his glass. "I'm sure you are."

"You know, *pretty* is overrated. It's not worth the price some girls pay for it."

"I most certainly agree." He nods, sipping his drink.

"Dr. Roth, I'm told you're an art aficionado."

"I am."

"Well," she says, making a gentle sweep with her hand, "which painting do you resonate with most?"

His eyes widen. "*Resonate!* And a fine vocabulary."

"Isn't it charming?" She grins. "My mother read *Anna Karenina* to me when I was six. She always said people tend to live at the level of their language."

"My, my!" he says.

"Well? Stop stalling, Doctor. Which painting?"

Dr. Roth glances around the gallery. He points to the corner. "I'm partial to Mr. Barlow's boxing series."

"Why?"

"Well," he says, staring at the painting. "because he connects me to a brutal world, a hostile environment I wouldn't normally know." He walks us over to a wounded boxer lying on the canvas. "Barlow's images are obviously born from personal experience, and his paint seems to drip with his own blood and sweat. These paintings are wild but learned, and I doubt any artist has ever depicted an athletic event with more truth, passion, and authority."

"Truth, passion, and authority," repeats Mimi.

"Yes. I look at his boxing series and I feel a shiver of recognition."

"Recognition?" repeats Mimi.

"Everyone's a fighter, young lady — in his or her own chosen arena."

Mimi clenches her fists and strikes a boxer's pose. "Ding! Ding! Ding!"

He smiles. "Mr. Barlow will be hanging in the contemporary wing of the Met some day."

Mimi tilts her head. "Will you be buying a painting this evening, Doctor?"

"Already have." He points to two paintings. "See the red dots? There and there."

Mimi smiles. "What a cool idea! This way they won't get lonely."

Dr. Roth raises his bushy eyebrows. "You seem to be a rather unique young lady. I'd buy you, if you were for sale."

"I'd look pretty damn ridiculous hanging on your living room wall," she says.

While they continue speaking, the blister inside my sock is throbbing. I keep searching the gallery for my dad. He promised he'd come.

"Where are you?" I whisper.

I turn and see him standing here.

"Nice game this afternoon!" he says.

"You were there?"

"In the stands, watching the whole time."

"Really?"

"I'm proud how you ran that end-sweep."

"You always enjoyed watching my games."

Dad grins. "Guess who's moving back to Closter next week."

"You?"

He nods. "You know that little blue house for sale on Closter Dock Road?"

Of course this conversation never really happens. He's standing here only in my imagination.

I watch the tuxedoed waiters walking around offering fruit and cheese — mushy cheese, crumbly cheese, smelly cheese. Red, blue, yellow, and white cheese. They're also handing out fat little stuffed mushrooms. Why would anyone put a mushroom in their mouth? It's fungus. I learned in science class that farms are now growing mushrooms from babies' diapers. That's a fact. I'm not eating fungus food. Give me a pig-in-a-blanket with yellow mustard. Or a Hershey bar with almonds.

Just then, a man wearing a tux approaches me. "Are you Matthew Watt?"

"And proud of it," I whisper.

"What?" he says, leaning closer.

"Nothing," I say. But those four words feel good coming out of my mouth.

"There's someone up front to see you."

Dad!

Chapter 56

I T'S MY ENGLISH TEACHER, MS. Hanover—her long, shiny, black hair flowing freely down behind her. She's wearing a red sleeveless gown that shows off her chiseled arms and BORN TO RAISE HELL tattoo. Her red high heels, nail polish and lipstick match flawlessly. Badass! Standing beside her is Funny Fred in his Scottish tweed and red polka-dot bowtie. What's their connection?

I hobble over.

Ms. Hanover points to my foot. "Limping?"

"Blister." I tell her about my football game that afternoon, but she interrupts me by putting her hands on my shoulders and kissing my cheek. Her kiss isn't for football or for tonight's show, but for my one-hundred-percent turnaround. "You've come a long way, Huckleberry."

"Huckleberry?"

She immediately slides into teacher mode, twisting her invisible Mark Twain moustache. "Huckleberry Finn kept runnin' away on his dang raft—but he always returned for my next chapter. Every now and then we all gotta escape. The world's full o' runaways. But we always gotta return for the next chapter."

I smile. "Ms. Hanover, I never told you this, but you're my favorite teacher." She smiles, twists her moustache, and winks. Suddenly, I feel awkward complimenting a teacher and open the brochure and point. "Ms. Hanover, why's there an extra painting?"

Funny Fred grabs the brochure, flips to the last page, and reads: "'*Sunset in Madrid* is on loan from the private collection of the former Queen of Spain.' That's where, Huckleberry. You neglected to read the penultimate paragraph. You don't mind if I use the word *penultimate*, do you?"

Hanover rolls her eyes. "Always the Princeton popinjay." She adds, "The Queen and Mr. Barlow, they had a thing. Old Benny got around."

"So now you're connected to European royalty!" grins Fred.

Ms. Hanover rolls her eyes.

Just then, I glance over Ms. Hanover's shoulder and my knees buckle. For a moment, I can't think, breathe, feel, or hear. No words, no warning, no nothing.

When I can breathe again, I get dizzy and start sweating. My grandmother is standing in front of *A Songwriter at Work.* To her right is a beautiful woman who looks like she just walked off the set of a TV soap opera — my mother.

Chapter 57

MY MOTHER'S EYES WIDEN AND her mouth drops open when she turns around and spots me. "Matthew!" She begins shoving her way through the crowd to embrace me.

I embrace her back. I'm a tough guy, but a year's a long time without a motherly hug.

I look at her face, red and teary, and remember all her Freudian slips. "Are you alright, Ma?"

"Yes. Are you?" We keep staring at each other. My feelings are all over the place, a mix of anger and happiness. It's pretty damn confusing.

"What am I doing here, right?" she finally says, wiping away her tears.

I look over at my grandmother who nods.

My mother hooks her arm around my arm. "Is there a quiet place we can sit and talk?"

"I'll wait here," says Gram.

We sit down in the hardback chairs in Karp's office. I cross my legs, fold my arms, and look at an empty box of Entenmann's donuts sitting on Karp's typewriter. My mother sits upright, reaches for my hands, and pulls them into her lap. "Once your grandmother told me about this show, I knew I had to be here," she explains. "I wanted my arrival to be a surprise, so she picked me up at LaGuardia this afternoon. Jack's still in Rome, tying up loose ends. He sends his best."

There's a differentness about her. Her hair is shorter, less twisty and coiffed. And she's wearing simple jeans and sneakers instead of her usual fashionable skirt and leather pumps. "Where's your father?" she asks. "Shouldn't he be here?"

I shrug. "He's coming later." I notice her face has no makeup. She always wears makeup. No perfume. She sighs and looks into my eyes. "Matthew, it's been over a year since Daniel…"

"Two years."

"It's been emotionally raw for us all, but it's time to move on."

I suddenly feel anger spurt up inside me. I look at the empty donut box. She grabs my chin and yanks my head back to face her. Her fingers press into my cheeks. "Listen, Matthew!" The wildness in her eyes finally subsides and she lets go of my jaw. "Matthew, what in hell do you have against me?" She was weepy a second ago, now she's crazy! "We need to talk — you and I." That's when she leans back, takes a deep breath and recounts the evening of May 15, at her favorite restaurant.

"You want to get a job?" my father said. "I can't be married to an interior decorator, for God's sake!"

"I need to find a job," my mother announced, placing the book she had been reading down on the pink tablecloth.

"You need to stay home with the boys is what you need," he said. "I married a wife, not an interior decorator."

"I'm becoming exactly the kind of woman I hated more than anything in the world."

"What's wrong with you?"

"I don't know."

"You're not going to take care of the boys anymore?"

"They're older now. They don't need me as much."

"They're still in school," he said.

"I'm tired," she sighed. "It's a different world today, dear. Everything's changing. Women are finding jobs and going to work."

My dad glared at her, and as he glared, he picked up her book from the table and threw it to the floor. "*The Feminine Mystique*! Everything's changed since you started reading this crap. One moment I'm living with a warm, caring wife who enjoys cooking dinner and taking care of our boys, and the next minute she wants to reinvent herself and become the damn breadwinner."

"It won't exactly be like that."

"I forbid it," announced my father.

"I have dreams and ambitions of my own," said my mother.

"You're staying home," he said.

"You're too controlling. I can't take it anymore."

"I said no!"

My mother finishes her story and looks at me with a tear-soaked face. "Matt, this past year I haven't been a very good mother. But the love I have for you comes from the deepest part of me and will never die. When my Daniel passed away…" She looks up to the ceiling and closes her eyes. "Something ripped inside me. No mother should have to…" She shakes her head, composes herself. "That's when your father and I slowly began to…disintegrate. I needed to hold on to something strong and — and, well, strong."

"Then Jack came along," I say.

She nods.

"You've been away for months," I say. A mother just doesn't do that.

"Yes. I've needed to be away. Forgive me." She leans forward, reaches again for my hands, squeezing them tight. "Please forgive me."

I forgave my father. Could I cave in and forgive my mother?

"Matt, I was shackled by the duties and responsibilities of being a good mother — diapers, bottles, attending school plays and baseball games. I'm proud of all that, but your father wanted a wife enslaved forever. Matt, I don't know if you're aware of this, but there's a significant age difference between your father and me — sixteen years. When you boys grew older, dreams and ambitions of my own began to stir inside me. I was still young and I needed to strike out on my own."

I nod.

"I loved your father. But he wanted to clip my wings and keep me prisoner in his arms forever. We'd be together today if only he had encouraged me to grow and find myself."

"And stop drinking."

She nods. "I was so much younger than your father, and I think he was fearful one day I'd find someone else. And I did…myself."

I'm doing a lot of nodding, so I just sit there and listen. I glance over at the empty donut box, and then look back at her.

She straightens up in her chair, smiles, and her arm reaches out to ruffle my hair. "Matt, I'm here now. I'm back where I belong — with you. I love you and will always love you. Do you think you can remember that? I'll always be proud to be your mother, but I'm also proud to have spread my wings and become an interior designer." I see the sad happiness in her eyes.

"Mom, I'm sorry about Daniel."

She pauses for a long time. Her face reddens, and she looks up at the ceiling again. She closes her eyes. "So am I."

"It must've been terrible."

She wipes new tears with a pink tissue she pulls from her purse. "Daniel was a beautiful boy. He had so much potential."

I look at a face haunted by loss and guilt. Daniel shattered her. But somehow, taking a year off seems to have made her stronger, calmer. We've all been Huckleberrys, escaping on our private rafts.

But she's returned for the next chapter.

I sit on the edge of my chair and study my feet. I'm damn good at anger and holding grudges. I can continue criticizing her—point by point—but what good would that do? It takes a strong kid to resist the temptation of anger. I'm a strong kid.

Suddenly, with alotta tears, I look up at my mother. The wounds of the past and a year's worth of anger begin to dissolve. After this adult conversation I've gotten to know her better. My mom and I might be broken, but broken can be repaired—just like Sailor Barlow's ripped canvases.

"I love you, Mom," I say, hugging her.

Suddenly, I hear loud applause…and a barking dog.

Chapter 58

AH! MATTY!" SHOUTS A LOUD voice. He walks toward me, and hugs me. "My boy!" he slurs. I look into the Champ's eyes and see joy and pride—it's a heart-felt happiness—something I had never seen before in his face. It's a look of pure joy that I'll never forget as long as I live.

The pretty woman standing beside his wheelchair is all dolled up in a green velvet dress, matching green shoes, and sparkly green eye shadow—Wanda. The guy beside her, wearing a purple suede jacket and jeans looks like a husband, but you never can be too sure about these things. The barking dog, jumping up and down, is the spitting image of Lavender—without a wiener sausage eye.

Wanda kisses my cheek, and then rubs off her lipstick. "Matthew, meet my husband, Lamar." We shake hands.

Wanda turns to the dog. "Matthew, meet Pork Chop. Pork Chop, Matthew."

"Chases squirrels," says the Champ with a smile.

"Pork Chop keeps Mr. Barlow company during his morning roadwork," says Wanda.

The Champ nods. His body is shaking, but less than before, and he's put on weight since leaving the hospital two months ago. His skin is pink and healthy and his eyes look clear and focused. The last time we were together he was thin, confused, and wearing my father's clothes.

"You look good, Champ," I say, patting his back.

Wanda nods. "It's a wonder what new meds and nontoxic paint'll do."

The Champ grins. "I paint good."

"Easy cleanup—except for clothing," says Wanda, pointing to a blue smudge on the Champ's brown pants.

"Shit!" he growls. "Sky spit on me."

I remember the first time I met the Champ. He was sitting on a stoop with paint splattered all over him. "Got a little yellow on your sleeve, Champ," I say, pointing.

He inspects his arm and shakes his head. "Field pissed on me."

Pork Chop barks. The Champ pets behind her ears and her pink tongue hangs out happily.

Wanda says, "You should see the mural Mr. Barlow be painting in the solarium."

The Champ nods. "Spanish skyscape."

"Beautiful blue sky and big fluffy clouds!" she says.

He pulls my arm. "Come see it."

"Of course!"

"We will." Mimi smiles, stepping forward. She tips her head gracefully and makes an elegant curtsy. "It's my honor to finally meet you, sir."

The Champ smiles and scratches his cauliflower ear.

"I'd love to see that beautiful blue sky and those big fluffy clouds."

The Champ looks at her and then me. "She's purty."

"And smart too—for a girl." She smiles.

"Honey," says Wanda to her husband, "I wanna show you something." She walks us over to *A Songwriter at Work*. "This be Matthew's father."

Lamar smiles big. "Far out! He here tonight?"

"He's coming," I say, nodding. But I'm having my doubts.

"Talented man," says Lamar. He begins whistling a few bars of "You're Mine Always."

"And your mother?" asks Wanda, looking around the gallery. "She here?"

"She's right here," says a smiling voice behind me.

Everyone shakes hands.

"Mrs. Watt," says Wanda, "I was Mr. Barlow's nurse at St. Vincent's. I wanna tell you how supportive Matt's been to Mr. Barlow. You should be very proud. All this year, he befriended a man in need. I been very impressed."

The Champ reaches out to shake my mother's hand. "Wish he was my son."

Pork Chop starts barking for attention.

Suddenly, someone pats my shoulder from behind.

Dad! I knew you'd come!

Chapter 59

I TURN AND SEE IVAN Karp smiling at me. He's wearing a black top hat instead of his Detroit Tigers cap. He takes the cigar from his mouth, hugs me, and quietly burps. "Damn donuts."

Flanking him is Kelly Talese, the host of *Lost Stars.*

"Step back! Step back!" orders Kelly, waving her arms. Dozens of reporters and photographers move back as she positions the Champ, me, and Mimi in front of her camera crew. After fifteen minutes of detailed instructions, she says, "Don't forget to give the TV audience a big happy smile!"

The crowd goes quiet.

This is all pretty cool!

"Okay! Quiet everyone!" says Kelly. "Ready. Set. Action!"

"Hello, I'm Kelly Talese, the host of *Lost Stars — Where are They Now?* Tonight we are at the OK Harris Gallery, located at 383 West Broadway in New York City. Before introducing tonight's featured guest, I want you to meet Matthew Watt and his young friend, Mimi Breedlove."

Mimi tips her head and curtsies.

"Matthew and Mimi are two high school students responsible for making tonight's gala affair possible. One afternoon, while walking in Manhattan, the observant Miss Breedlove spotted an inconspicuous 'seat cushion' lying on the sidewalk. She picked it up and, well, that seat cushion happened to be hidden treasure — one of Mr. Barlow's lost paintings — and it's hanging on the wall right over there!"

The crowd turns to where she points.

"Matthew Watt reunited Mr. Barlow with the rest of these exquisite paintings we see here tonight. They were hidden inside — of all places — a kitchen table! In appreciation, Mr. Barlow has appointed Matthew the beneficiary of his estate."

Everyone looks at me as if I was someone special, which, of course I'm not.

She hands the microphone to a smiling Ivan Karp who begins to speak strong and clear. I can tell he's enjoying every minute of this. "The topsy-turvy art world has accepted, willingly or not, Christo's silliness, Andy Warhol's vapidity, and the sheer nothingness of Yves Klein. This shock-art, in my humble opinion, is cultural pollution. Tonight, however, is a joyous occasion. Tonight, we celebrate Benny Barlow's pure passion and artistry on twenty-two brilliant canvases." He hands the mic back to Talese.

"Tonight's 'Lost Star' is the inimitable Benny 'Sailor' Barlow! At the tender age of sixteen Benny entered the professional boxing ranks and climbed the fistic ladder to become the tenth undisputed light heavyweight champion of the world. After retiring from the ring, he reinvented himself as a painter. Art is a love affair, and that's precisely what he has given us this evening — his love and passion. So, tonight we recognize Mr. Barlow's sensational climb up the artistic ladder, a feat which would have gone tragically unnoticed, if it were not for the devotion and conviction of these two brave and resourceful youngsters."

Polite applause.

The camera turns back to Mr. Karp. "Matthew and Mimi, your bravery and commitment have led to the discovery of priceless paintings by a man whom the art world will soon regard as the modern-day Rembrandt of primitive art." He then raises the Champ's arm above his head, like a referee declaring the winner of a championship bout.

The crowd applauds. Pork Chop barks.

Mr. Karp, basking in the spotlight, goes on for a few more embarrassing sentences about how wonderful a kid I am. But none of it is true. I'm just a scared boy who played hooky from school and stole money from my grandmother. I just got lucky to hang out with the Champ. I'm grateful for every single second of it.

Then come Kelly Talese's questions: How did you meet tonight's guest? Can you describe the kitchen table? Who is Lavender? Are you really George Watts's son?

"In closing," she says, "Matthew, tell us what meeting tonight's *Lost Stars* guest has meant to you." She holds the microphone close to my face and waits for my answer.

I freeze.

I hear coughing. I hear whispering. I hear my own silence.

Kelly smiles and asks the question differently. "In other words, Matthew, briefly tell us what you have learned from meeting Benny Barlow."

I look at the painting of a wounded fighter lying on the mat. I look at the painting of my father hunched over a piano. I look at the painting of a small boy reading a letter. I look at the Champ's scarred face and cauliflower ear. I then turn to the camera, clear my throat, and grab the mic. "I learned the two hardest things to handle in life are success and failure." I leave it at that. And I didn't stutter once.

People clap politely.

Pork Chop barks.

After fielding a million more questions and being photographed a few zillion times, everyone walks away and begins eating cheese and mushrooms again. I turn to Ms. Hanover. "What's a beneficiary of an estate?"

She shakes her head and frowns. "If you hadn't skipped school so much last year, you'd know."

"It means," says Mimi, "all the money from Mr. Barlow's paintings will be set aside for his care, but afterwards, all proceeds go to you."

"Ah," I say, nodding. "Now I get it."

But I don't, really. I'm still confused.

"Proceeds?" I whisper.

"Money, dummy," Mimi whispers.

My mouth drops open. I look at the Champ smiling up at me. He reaches for my hand and squeezes it.

At the end of the evening, when the food is finished and everyone's gone, there's still a small group of us puttering around. Except for the blister drooling inside my wet sock, and my father not coming, I'm feeling pretty good.

"So," asks my mother, "when will Mr. Barlow's episode air?"

"March," says Mimi, petting Pork Chop's head.

I look at the Champ and realize March is when I first met him. I was a confused kid running away from school seeking serenity. Instead, I found an old demented monster with a paint-stained shirt who called

211

me George. Yeah, a lot has happened this year: red roses and thin pizza, a spitball hitting my ear, standing up to a bully, getting punched by a world champion boxer, connecting to boxing royalty, crying in a hospital, The Hump, finding a girlfriend with a dog whistle, finding valuable paintings, finding my lost father, and reconnecting with my mother.

And I found myself.

I look at Mimi, put my arms around her, and hug her tight.

"What's that for?" she says.

"Everything."

My mother, Gram, Wanda, and Lamar are putting on their winter coats.

Lamar says to the Champ, "I'm no art critic, Champ, but when I seen you fight in Sunnyside Garden, your left hook be pretty as a picture! You could hang that hook up in The Met it be so pretty!"

The Champ grins sleepily. He lifts his left hand and makes a fist.

"I'm serious, man! You a freakin' monster that night! I remember your physique—wide shoulders and itty bitty waist. Your back be an isosceles triangle!"

"An isosceles what?" says Wanda, slipping on her green overcoat.

"You know, a triangle that, uh…"

"That's equal on at least two sides," I clarify.

Mimi looks at me, stunned.

"I learned that in geometry class." I smile.

It feels good to be smart—for a change.

Epilogue

I T'S SATURDAY AFTERNOON IN DECEMBER, overcast and cold, and I'm sitting on the park bench at 65th and Columbus Avenue waiting for my dad to show.

He's late.

Last Saturday he was sick and couldn't make it, but he promised he'd be here today. I know everyone has problems and my dad is no exception. But it's getting chilly, and I'm hoping like anything he'll come soon.

I'm glad I'm wearing my football jacket. It's nice and warm, unlike the weather.

A gray squirrel lingers close by until it's clear I'm a waste of time. Then he darts off.

I sit back on the bench and hum my father's song while I wait.

I hum three more songs. Each was a big hit on the *Billboard* charts two decades ago.

I look up and down the street.

No dad.

So I start my old waiting game. I count: 10...9...8...7...6...5...4...3...2...1... My father is coming around the corner right now!

I do that ten times till I get tired.

"I'm here, Dad," I say softly.

The sun is high in the sky, but it will be dipping behind the buildings soon.

Some pigeons come by to see if I'm feeding anyone. I am not, and they waddle off. They should have checked with the squirrel.

I'm getting the bad feeling Dad isn't gonna show.

Life has too many complications. And not all connections connect.

I look up and down Columbus Avenue. I lean back on the bench and wait.

"I'm here, Dad," I repeat softly.

10...9...8...7...6...5...4...3...2...1... My father is coming around the corner right...now.

About the Author

PETER WOOD has long been acknowledged as a heavyweight champion of boxing literature. He is the author of *Confessions of a Fighter – Battling Through the Golden Gloves* and *A Clenched Fist – The Making of a Golden Gloves Champion*, two memoirs published by Ringside Books.

His first book, *To Swallow a Toad*, an adult novel, was a runner-up in an Ohio new-fiction competition, and later re-titled *Confessions of a Fighter*. *Confessions* was optioned for film by Steve Nicoleides, *(When Harry Met Sally, Boyz n the Hood, and A Few Good Men.)*

Peter, a tough middleweight Golden Gloves Finalist in Madison Square Garden, was asked to represent America in the 1976 Maccabean Games held in Tel Aviv, Israel. He declined and decided to begin hitting the books instead. He graduated from Fordham University in 1976 with a BA in Communications; Ohio State in 1984 with a BS in Education, and The College of New Rochelle with a MS in School Administration in 1990.

But Peter was always writing. His follow-up book, *A Clenched Fist*, written with the same honest, hardcore prose he is known for, was completed while teaching English, and coaching football, baseball, and boxing at White Plains High School.

In 2012, he made his off-Broadway acting debut in *Kid Shamrock* at The TADA Theater, and in 2017 he appeared in the New York City indie film, *The Expediter*. In addition to acting, Peter has written two full-length plays, *Candy Bars* and *Our Similarities Are Different* — both produced in regional theatre in Westchester, New York.

Peter also switched canvases, becoming a painter who has enjoyed numerous art shows in Manhattan, Easthampton, NY, and the Midwest. One of Peter's paintings was featured in the Katonah Museum of Art.

Peter and his work have appeared in a variety of media outlets including a guest column in *The New York Times*, interviews on ESPN, and on *The Sally Jessie Raphael Show*, WOR's *The Joey Reynolds Show*, and WFUV. His articles have appeared in *Commonweal, America, Ring, Boxing Illustrated, Westchester Magazine, Chicken Soup for the Soul, Proof*, Boxing. com and TheSweetScience.com. His feature article in *Sporting Classics* has been anthologized in its 25th anniversary leather-bound edition featuring their 40 finest pieces of writing.

Born in New York City and raised in New Jersey, Peter is married to his artist wife, Susan, they have a talented daughter, Zoe, who is now a proud Bowdoin College graduate.

Connect with Peter

Sign up for Peter's newsletter at
www.peterwwood.com/free

To find out more information visit his website:
www.peterwwood.com

Facebook:
www.facebook.com/pete.wood.1671

Get Book Discounts and Deals

One Last Thing ...

Thank you for reading! If you enjoyed this book, I'd be very grateful if you'd post a short review on Amazon. I read every comment personally and am always learning how to make this book even better. Your support really does make a difference.

Search for *The Boy Who Hit Back* by Peter Wood to leave your review.

Thanks again for your support!

Made in the USA
Coppell, TX
01 November 2019